Hair Today, Dead Tomorrow

A Spring Harbor Cozy Mystery

Amber Crewes

Pen-n-a-Pad Publishing

Other books in the Spring Harbor Series

A Spring Harbor Cozy Mystery

Book One

1

Summer Snow dropped her suitcase and pulled a wayward curl out of her eyes for the hundredth time since landing.

"That's it!" If Aunt Clara didn't show up soon, she was going to dig through her bag for either a bobby pin or scissors. At this point, she didn't care which.

Where was Aunt Clara, anyway? Summer looked at her phone, hoping to find a message, although she knew her aunt well enough to know she'd never text. Instead, she found a message from her best friend, Vanessa.

'*You alive?*'

Summer smiled wide, even as she rolled her eyes and replied, '*Nope.*'

'*K. Just checking!*'

Vanessa knew Summer was scared of flying, but these kinds of texts had been coming more often since 'the incident.'

> *'Just waiting for Aunt Clara to pick me up. How's...where are you again?'*

> *'Paris! Girl, you know I'm doing that winter handbag shoot'*

'Totally forgot' Summer lied. How could she forget Paris?

> *'I'm sure Paris has nothing on Spring Harbor! You go find yourself a hot surfer dude to help you forget all your troubles!'*

> *'A dude is the last thing I need in my life!'*

Just then, a cloud of Jovan Musk perfume came right at her and she smiled. Aunt Clara must be single-handedly keeping that company afloat.

"There you are!" Aunt Clara emerged from the cloud with her arms outstretched. "I've been looking all over for you! How was your flight? Are you feeling OK? You know...after everything?"

Summer grabbed her aunt in a bear hug to keep her from continuing with the line of questioning. Word travels fast in the Newberg-Snow family. "I'm good, Aunt Clara. How are you? Where are you off to after this?"

Aunt Clara just shrugged. "I can't keep track. It's on my calendar at home. We can check when we get back. But first, I want to show my beautiful niece off! What do you say we run by the main strip and take a few laps?"

Summer groaned. "I'm not a prize poodle, Aunt Clara. Not that I'd win any right now." She grabbed her shirt and made a show of sniffing it. "I think the air on that plane has been recycled a few too many times."

"Aww," Aunt Clara said, pinching Summer's cheek like she was still a precocious child. "Cute and funny. You're gonna make someone a great wife someday."

Summer picked up her suitcase and started walking. "Says the woman who never married."

"Well, I don't have your sense of humor, or those curls! How did you get your hair to do that, anyway?" Aunt Clara tugged on one of the offending strands of hair.

"Spackle."

Aunt Clara laughed and clicked her key fob as soon as they stepped out of the airport. A bright yellow VW Beetle chirped in response.

"You got a punch buggy?"

"Isn't it adorable?"

"You know we're gonna put eyelashes on this thing before I leave, right?"

"Obviously! I was just waiting for you!"

Summer knew it wasn't exactly true. Neither of them had been expecting 'the incident', which left her with too much time and a lot of big life decisions on her hands. But still, when her mom called last week and said Aunt Clara would be staying a while in Spring Harbor, CA, it seemed like the perfect time for a vacation...all the way across the country felt just far enough from her problems to be a good idea.

"It's not as warm as I expected," Summer said, partly because she meant it and partly to keep the conversation light. One ill-timed pause and Aunt Clara would've surely started prodding.

"Isn't it lovely? That's why I picked this town. It's so picturesque and full of life, but high enough up the map to beat the heat. Plus, now that it's fall, we get to watch the leaves change together."

Summer looked at her aunt, all five-foot-two of her, and felt like she was finally home. "I can't wait."

———

A few years ago, when Summer's mom told her Aunt Clara was selling everything and driving across the country in an RV, she wasn't sure what she pictured that looking like, but it definitely wasn't the scene before her now. Instead of rows of neat, tiny RVs full of quiet old people, the Wheels Up! RV Park was crawling with kids and families. There was yelling and laughing and barking, all flying past Aunt Clara's punch buggy as they pulled up to a massive RV with —of course—yellow pin-striping.

"Wow, Aunt Clara. Do you just...drive this thing up in there when it's time to go?"

"No, silly." Aunt Clara chuckled as she got out of the car and pushed a button on the side of the RV. A string of lights bordering the awning blinked on, as did several inside the camper. "That wouldn't leave me much room for my toys."

"Toys?" Summer asked with trepidation.

But the gleam in Aunt Clara's eyes turned it to pure fear. "What did you do?"

"I made sure I have what I need wherever I end up." She led Summer to the back door, which opened onto a garage-looking room with a four-wheeler, skis, a boogie board, and so much more.

"You're gonna kill yourself with all this stuff, Aunt Clara. You're-"

"If you say 'too old' I'm taking you right back to the airport." She was serious too, hand on the hip serious.

"I would never. But...be careful."

It was Aunt Clara's turn to roll her eyes. "Always."

A dog started barking like crazy behind them, and Summer turned to see an older gentleman in a tight blue Polo shirt clearly staring at them. Then, two kids ran by with a frisbee and a ball, causing the dog to give chase. Squeals of laughter echoed inside the metal room.

"Is it always this...lively?"

Aunt Clara waved at the older gentleman and closed the door. "It's the Fall Festival. Apparently, it's a big deal around here. Even the locals come stay at the park for the weekend."

They walked through to the rest of the camper, which was still larger than expected, though so full of stuff, Summer didn't know where to sit. Or where she would sleep.

"Um." Summer looked around the living area at all the knick knacks and camping equipment. "Maybe I should get a room in town. I don't want to put you out."

"Oh, nonsense." Aunt Clara waved her away and started moving stacks of papers off the counter. It looked like she picked up every flyer at every tourist trap she ever visited. "There's no place open now, anyway. Not with the leaves changing. Besides," she said, holding up one of the many flyers. "If you're not here, how will we ever participate in all these fun activities together?"

Aunt Clara handed Summer the flyer, which had at least a hundred activities printed on it. One in particular was circled in bright red.

"A Crazy Hair Contest?" Summer gave her aunt a sidelong glance.

"You didn't think I invited you here for nothing, did you?" And there it was, that same gleam in Aunt Clara's eyes that meant she was up to something naughty. "Now, get freshened up so I can show you around town before you turn back into a pumpkin."

"Are you insinuating I'm Cinderella's coach?"

"Oh, is that what the pumpkin is? What does Cinderella turn back into?"

"A very sad girl..."

"Well," Aunt Clara said, ushering her toward what she hoped was a bathroom. "We can't have that, now can we? No sad girls allowed in my camper. Fix your face and get ready to paint this town red!"

"Fine, but I'm not staying out all night. I've heard wild stories about you retirees." Summer closed the bathroom door and turned on the water.

Through the door, she heard Aunt Clara laugh again. "Child, I could put every one of those stories to shame."

"With Mr. Tight Polo?"

"What? Who? Carl? No...he's just a friendly neighbor."

Summer grinned and mocked her aunt's fake innocent response. "What? Who? Carl?"

"Hush!" Aunt Clara walked away, and Summer was sure she heard the embarrassment in her voice.

"Get it, Aunt Clara! At least one of us is." Then she shook her head, reminding herself that she was very much not looking for a man. She came here for some R & R. A nice, quiet few days with her Aunt Clara to chase away the horrors of the real world.

2

Twenty minutes and several knocks on the bathroom door later, Summer emerged feeling somewhat refreshed and a lot less self-conscious. She wasn't ready to hear the same questions over and over again, the one old people loved to ask.

So what do you do for a living?

Are you seeing anyone?

When are you going to get married and have some kids?

Summer Snow, huh? What's your favorite season?

It was enough to make her try to step back into the bathroom, if it wasn't for Aunt Clara's tiny foot blocking the door. For someone so compact, she sure was strong.

"The sooner you let me do this, the sooner it will be over. Besides, don't you want to go check out the pool? And the concession stand has the best nachos!"

"I'm not twelve, Aunt Clara," Summer groaned, though she secretly hoped the night ended with nachos.

Summer straightened the front of her t-shirt, a stalling method since that's what she'd spent the last few minutes doing in the bathroom.

"So that's what you went with?" Aunt Clara asked.

Summer shrugged.

"It says, 'Stop saying words to me.'"

Summer raised her eyebrows. An answer and a challenge.

"You're too much like your mother, girl." Aunt Clara took Summer's hand and pulled her out the door.

Outside, as if waiting for them. Mr. Carl stood from the picnic table he'd been sitting at. His smile was wide and inviting, and Aunt Clara went to it like a moth to a flame. "Carl, I want you to meet my niece, Summer. She's visiting from…"

"Out of town." Summer didn't want people knowing she'd been in Atlanta. Once word got out about *the incident*, they might put two and two together. She came here for an escape, as much as to visit Aunt Clara. She couldn't risk the story following her. Not yet.

Carl put out his hand for Summer to shake. He had a firm, honest grip. Some of her concerns melted away instantly. Even as he greeted her, he couldn't take his eyes off Aunt Clara. The poor man was smitten. And when he said in his deep, gruff voice, "Summer. That's a lovely name for a lovely girl. Now I see where your aunt gets it," he still held Aunt Clara's gaze.

Aunt Clara gave Carl a light smack on the arm. "Oh, Carl, you are incorrigible."

"Thank you for noticing." He smiled and kissed the top of her hand like they were the only two people in the whole campground.

Summer kind of wished they were. She felt like she was intruding and took a subconscious step back.

Finally, Carl turned his broad, white smile toward her. "You married?"

Summer took a deep breath. *Let the questions begin.*

But before she could give one of her already prepared answers, Aunt Clara said, "Why Carl, so easily swayed. I didn't take you for that kind of man."

His deep brown eyes were back on Aunt Clara and Summer had no idea that old people could smolder, but he certainly was. "My sweet Clara. I could never. But I do have a son who would love..."

"I'm fine," Summer cut in. "I...I don't need a man in my life right now. And from the looks of you two, your son might very well be my cousin one day."

Carl's face lit up and Aunt Clara shot Summer an unreadable look.

"So," Summer added, to please, please change the subject. "How long have you been here, Mr. Carl?"

He turns back to her. "Mr. Carl? Where are you from, girl?"

Crap!

"You don't have an accent, but..."

Aunt Clara put a hand on his arm. "Mr. Jacobson's a retired detective. And Summer's from down South."

From Carl's nod, that was explanation enough.

Summer relaxed again. "So, Mr. Jacobson, how long-"

"No, no, that won't do. Carl is fine. Plain old—but not *too* old—Carl." He said the last part with a wink in Aunt Clara's direction. "I've been in California since the 80s, but here in Spring Harbor only since '07."

"Wow, here in the park?" Summer looked around at all the RVs, noticing that some looked to be more permanent than others.

"No, this is just the past couple of years. After my wife..." He trailed off, then cleared his throat. "The house was just too big."

Aunt Clara's hand was still on his arm and Summer saw her give it a soft squeeze.

"Don't know how much longer I'll be here, though." He heaved a big sigh.

Summer looked at Aunt Clara, wondering just how serious she was with this man. Were they planning to RV off into the sunset together? After sixty years of the single life, she couldn't imagine Aunt Clara settling down. But still, her hand never moved from Carl's arm, and his eyes never moved from her.

The uneasy, intruding feeling crept back up Summer's spine.

It was Aunt Clara who finally spoke. "There are rumors that Councilman Harding is going to rezone the park so he can sell it to a strip mall developer."

"Oh, that's terrible."

Carl and Aunt Clara nodded in unison, matching somber looks on their faces.

Summer watched them with more than a little concern. For someone who flits from town to town, Aunt Clara sure was interested in this one all of a sudden.

———

It took a while to get out of the RV park, between Aunt Clara exchanging lovey dovey looks with Carl, and the sheer number of new friends she'd made in her short time living there. But they finally made it to town, where the real introductions began.

It was a swirl of names, faces, and quaint architecture until Summer's stomach growled enough to warn both of them that the evening was coming to an end. They wound up at a lovely little cafe in the heart of town, Cafe Cali. The decor matched the rest of the town, nestled somewhere between beach chic and cozy cottage. Summer wasn't sure how they pulled it off, but it worked perfectly.

"Clara!" A short, perky girl came running toward their table. "Where have you been hiding? I got the new Campfire collection in." The woman looked to be about twenty-five, close in age to Summer, but barely as tall as Aunt Clara. Her short, choppy brunette waves swished over her shoulder as she bent down to hug Aunt Clara.

Strangely, Summer didn't feel an ounce of jealousy at this woman's closeness to her aunt. The giant smile and equally giant doe eyes on her face made it impossible.

Aunt Clara broke out of the hug and gestured toward Summer. "Alex, this is my niece, Summer. She's visiting from out of town." They'd repeated this scene so many times, Aunt Clara got the hang of not saying anything more.

"Oh, nice to meet you!" Alex jutted out a hand for Summer, which she took. "Your aunt told me so much about you."

"Did she?"

"All good, of course! Oh, you two look so much alike!" Alex let go of Summer's hand to clap hers together in excitement. "I'm so glad you're here! We need fresh meat in this place."

Summer's brows raised.

Aunt Clara laughed and patted Summer's arm. "I think she meant new blood."

As if that was better.

Alex didn't seem to notice or care. She just kept chattering on. "This is perfect! Clara tells me you're a hairdresser." She puffed up the ends of her hair. "We could really use you around here. Rumor has it Mrs. Beesley's kids are forcing her to retire. There might be an-"

"Thank you," Summer said in an attempt to stop the barrage of information. Then she leveled a stern look at Aunt Clara, who only sipped her water. What, exactly, had Aunt Clara been telling people about her? She hadn't worked in a hair salon in years.

Though, if she was honest with herself, the mention of a hair salon did make her fingers twitch and tingle. And visions of running around a bright, quaint little hair salon that was all hers...It sounded too good to be true.

Aunt Clara, no doubt catching the glaze over her features, said, "Sounds like fate to me."

"*Feels* more like a set-up to me," Summer scolded.

"Why, Summer Snow, whatever do you mean?" Aunt Clara clutched at nonexistent pearls.

Alex clapped her hands again. "Summer Snow. OMG that's so adorable! I love it! And I'm Alexandra Mays. That sounds like fate, too! But May is Spring, though, right? We just need to find someone named Autumn and we'd be unstoppable."

Summer had to admit Alex's joy was infectious. The stress of the past couple of months started to ease away as Summer took a seat beside her. "And what do you do? What's a Campfire collection?"

"Socks!" Alex said the word as if it was a totally normal response to 'What do you do?' When Summer didn't know what to say to that, Alex continued. "I run a little sock shop on Main. Total tourist trap, but I love it!"

"Interesting. What's it-"

"Sole Mate!" Alex didn't even wait for Summer to finish.

She had to admit; it was catchy.

"It's not far from the salon..." Alex said, with a side eye toward Aunt Clara.

"You don't say?" Summer replied with a much different type of side eye toward Aunt Clara.

"But..." Alex said, then caught herself.

And despite her reservations about being thrown to the lions right now, Summer couldn't help but ask, "But what?"

Alex bit her cheek.

Aunt Clara said, "Spring Harbor only has one real estate agent."

Then both women said, "Drew Harding."

"That didn't sound ominous at all."

Alex shook her head slowly. "He's a piece of work. He's been involved in so many bad deals...well, bad for us. Never bad for him and his clients. They have ways of making people sell."

Another shiver went up Summer's spine. "Isn't he...part of the government? Didn't Carl say..."

Alex clapped again. "Carl," she cooed, and gave Aunt Clara a nudge. Then she looked back at Summer. "Yes, he's a city councilman, but he still kept his day job."

Summer nodded. "So, him and his partners wanting to buy the Wheels Up..."

Alex groaned. "Marsha Peterson and her daughter Jennifer West."

Aunt Clara said, "Don't forget Mario," with a wink toward Alex.

Summer turned to her aunt. "What was that for?"

Alex laughed. "Let's just say Marsha's third husband is... super hot...super dumb...and probably the same age as her daughter."

Summer made a face that had Aunt Clara and Alex both nodding in agreement. Whatever daydreams she'd allowed herself to have about opening her own hair salon faded with each passing moment. It was beginning to look like she'd be back in her boring, horrible old life sooner than later.

3

"**A**re you sure you want to do this?" Summer hovered in the front door of the RV. She had a slapdash bag of hair styling equipment slung over her shoulder, things she'd borrowed from Alex, Aunt Clara, and a couple of people Carl had recruited. It was like she had a whole styling team at her disposal, a thought that exhilarated and terrified her.

"Stop stalling," Aunt Clara said, coming out of the bathroom in a modest robe. She pulled it tight and slipped on her red sandals. Her long, luxurious white hair fell almost to her waist. It was the first time Summer had seen it down in at least a decade. "You've had two days to get your head in the game. Now it's time to show this town what you're made of."

"Town?" Summer gulped. This Crazy Hair Contest was supposed to be a fun little campground family bonding activity. What did the whole town have to do with it?

"Oh, stop. It's become sort of a tradition around here. That's all." Aunt Clara didn't give her much more time to fret before swinging open the door.

Carl was standing on the edge of her 'yard' and let out a whistle.

"Carl, you scoundrel. I'm not even done up yet." Aunt Clara patted her hair, more demurely than Summer had ever seen her.

Carl tore his eyes off Aunt Clara and smiled at Summer. "You guys have this thing in the bag. With your skills and your lovely model, these other guys don't stand a chance."

Summer was immune to Carl's sweet talk by now, but she couldn't help but wonder if she really did have a chance. It was a small town fun contest, sure. But the thought of winning something with her hairstyles was invigorating. When she'd told Vanessa about it yesterday, she'd been embarrassed to care so much about something so small. But Vanessa had been ecstatic. She even made Summer promise to send her pictures.

That was a loaded demand, considering Vanessa's job was Influencer. She had a massive social media following. Knowing a picture of her hairstyle might end up plastered all over the internet was nerve-racking.

Before she could refuse to take one more step, Carl and Aunt Clara had dragged her halfway across the campground to the Rec Center.

People were scattered everywhere inside and outside of the building. It looked like half of them had started their styles hours ago and were nearly finished, while she and Aunt Clara were just getting started.

"Here's where I leave you two lovely ladies. Knock 'em dead!" Carl patted them both on the arm and pointed to a picnic table off to the left. "I'll be over there."

A tall woman in a flowing overcoat led them to a row of tables to get set up. Beside them, an older woman was fixing a young girl's hair into something like a beehive.

"Clara," the woman said, barely looking up.

"Ramona."

From Aunt Clara's tone, Summer knew better than to ask. Instead, she hurriedly began teasing and spraying Aunt Clara's hair while checking out the competition.

There was a woman in a full bohemian dress with leaves and twigs binding her hair. It was actually quite lovely how some of the auburn strands cascaded down her back. A few tables away, a very handsome man sat perfectly still while a young girl of about seven put butterfly clips all over his hair. The more she looked, the more she noticed a theme.

"Aunt Clara, is this for children?"

"What? No. Of course not. Ramona over here is at least ninety."

Ramona, who had definitely been listening, huffed and turned her model's chair away.

Summer combed one nuisance knot a bit too hard, jerking Aunt Clara's head in warning.

Ignoring her, Aunt Clara still chuckled under her breath.

It took another twenty minutes to finish Aunt Clara's hair. By the time they were done, most of the room had cleared out. Only they and the handsome man remained.

A woman came in just as someone said over the speaker that it was time to line up for the judges. The woman, tall and wide, lumbered up to them and inspected Summer's work. When Summer got a good look at her in the mirror, she took back her earlier assessment that what the Ramona woman had been giving the girl was a beehive.

This...magnificent structure atop this new woman's head was the beehive of all beehives. A swirling, stiff mass of jet black hair towered so high above them that the mirror couldn't even capture the whole thing.

The woman looked from Aunt Clara's hair to the handsome man and made a noise under her breath.

"Amazing isn't it, Gertie?" Aunt Clara asked as she stood. "If you'll excuse me, I have a contest to win."

The woman only made another snide noise, which had the handsome man fleeing.

Summer stood alone in the dressing room with this formidable woman, with only a hair dryer for protection.

Why she felt she needed protection, she didn't know. But she also didn't let go.

———

After an awkward staring contest with the beehive woman, Summer was saved by the intercom. The crowd of people lined up along the perimeter of the Rec Center as the models made their way across the stage.

Summer arrived at the door just in time to see Aunt Clara strut toward the judges. She'd removed her robe to reveal a loose brown, shimmering dress with glittering leaves of gold and orange sprinkled across the front and back. With her arms out, it looked like a forest floor come to life. And on her head, her white-gray hair had been transformed into a majestic oak. The trunk spread out into a twisting root system and the crown was an array of red and light green leaves. More leaves, gold and orange like those of her dress, seemed to fall with every step.

Summer bet if Aunt Clara and the beehive woman stood toe to toe, her tree might have been taller. With a glance in the other woman's direction, she was certain they'd just had the same thought.

It only took a few moments for the judges to confer and crown Summer the winner. She had to admit, none of the other styles came close to what she'd created. And she was proud to send several pictures to Vanessa.

'Wow! Did you do all that yourself?'

'Aunt Clara's hair is very malleable. It was nothing'

'We'll see about that'

She didn't have time to worry about what that meant before an uneasy feeling made her look up from her phone. Several of the older women standing around the Rec Center were glaring at her. Two she recognized, Ms. Beehive and

Ramona. Now, seeing them that close together, she noticed the family resemblance. Sisters probably.

As if catching her staring, they both walked toward Summer and Aunt Clara with near matching scowls.

"This isn't good," Summer whispered.

"Psh, they're harmless."

"Congratulations," Ramona said, not meaning it in the slightest.

Beehive made another slow trip around Aunt Clara, like she'd done in the dressing room. "Creative."

"Thank you," Aunt Clara and Summer said in unison.

Then Aunt Clara put her hand on Summer's shoulder and added, "You'd be lucky to have her."

Summer's brows furrowed.

So did the woman's, before stepping closer still.

Summer scanned the room for...anything. Anyone to save her. But they were alone. Even the hot guy and his little girl who had been hanging back—Summer had hoped he was going to approach her. Instead, she got these two vipers. How did she get herself backed into a corner like this? Like prey?

"Yes, well..." Beehive said, tugging at a falling leaf of gold painted hair, testing the structural integrity of Summer's work. "Maybe it's time to update the rules to only allow children to participate. Seems unfair, doesn't it?"

Summer risked a glance behind the woman to her sister. She didn't think they'd have that same opinion if her beehive had won.

Aunt Clara only nodded, the tree of hair atop her head bowing in the sun setting through the window. "I agree. Two categories, one for the children and one for adults. Next year."

Ramona nearly gasped at Aunt Clara's use of 'next year,' as if she didn't expect to still have to deal with her in a year's time.

Summer also gasped. Since her retirement, Aunt Clara hadn't stayed in one place longer than a month.

Then Beehive's lips tightened into a straight line and she sighed. "If there is a next year."

All three old women nodded in agreement, finally finding common ground.

Aunt Clara broke their silent truce by saying, "Something needs to be done about Mr. Harding and the Peterson ladies."

"Indeed," Beehive said before a final look over Aunt Clara's hairstyle, then a passing glance at Summer.

Ramona, however, added one final shot across the bow, saying over her shoulder, "Seems we have a few people who need something done."

Once they were out of earshot, Summer grabbed her aunt. "What was all that about?"

"What? Them buying this place out to flatten it? Carl and I already told you..."

Summer shook her head and leveled a stern look on Aunt Clara. "First of all, Carl and I? What's gotten into you? And second, not the RV park. Those women? I've never seen you so catty."

Aunt Clara's cheeks turned red. "Ramona and Gertrude Beesley. Two of the loveliest women you've ever met."

"That Ramona hates your guts."

Now her cheeks darkened, but for a much different reason. "She had a thing for Carl before I blew into town." With that, Aunt Clara actually started strutting away, hips swinging.

Summer stood behind her in awe, shaking her head. Awe of the confidence, and the high school shenanigans. Then Aunt Clara's words sank in. 'The Beesley women.'

Mrs. Beehive is *the* Mrs. Beesley with the hair salon she was supposed to be schmoozing. Not trading verbal jabs. Looks like that whole business plan just flew out the window.

4

The next day, all Summer wanted was to relax before her time with Aunt Clara came to an end. Her return flight was in three days, and Aunt Clara had a trip to Colorado on her calendar.

Summer stretched, amazed that she could be laying out by a pool in late October. It was unseasonably warm already in Spring Harbor, CA. But the Wheels Up RV Park also kept their pool inside a clear plastic building. It reminded Summer of a greenhouse, and she felt like a lazy little flower, opening up toward the sun that morning. Nothing was going to dampen her mood.

"All I'm saying is, I should go talk to Gertie, make things right," Aunt Clara said for the hundredth time.

Except that.

"It's fine, Aunt Clara. When I got on the plane the other day, I wasn't planning on making a life here. And when I get back on it in a few more days, I'll forget all about it." It wasn't a total lie. She enjoyed this time with Aunt Clara.

She would never forget that. And winning the Crazy Hair Contest, she'd definitely never forget that.

Not with Vanessa's post blowing up. Summer only had socials to follow Vanessa, to support her best friend. But almost overnight, Summer herself now had thousands of followers, all begging for more pics.

'*What happened?*' Summer had texted Vanessa when her phone went crazy with notifications in the middle of the night.

'*They love your hairdo!*'

'*How do they know it's mine?*'

'*I tagged you silly. Seriously, you're too young to be this clueless about social media, especially with me as your BFF!*'

'*I know what tagging is!!*' She just forgot it was a thing. If she'd known it would garner this much attention, she never would have sent the pic. If Mr. DeVilla found out where she was...

"Ladies!"

Summer snapped out of her doom spiral and opened her eyes to find Carl standing over them, grinning from ear to ear. On anyone else, it would be gross, but Summer caught the slight change in Aunt Clara's posture. She was digging it.

"Carl," Aunt Clara said, coyly. "To what do we owe this honor?"

"It's my honor, really." He held up his hand and waved a thick little booklet. "You two took off so fast last night, you forgot your prize."

It was true. After the cat fight, neither of them felt very festive. Summer hadn't thought about the prize, or the fact that people might be waiting to see the winning hairstyle up close.

Aunt Clara took the booklet and passed it to Summer. "Sorry, we had a run in with your girlfriend."

Summer's brows shot up and Carl's fell, along with the corners of his lips. "How many times do I have to tell you..."

"Relax," Aunt Clara said with a Cheshire grin. "I'm just giving you a hard time. But we did run into the lovely Beesley ladies after the contest. Didn't feel much like celebrating after that."

"Yeah, they have that effect on people. Gertie's not that bad if she'd just get out from under Ramona's thumb."

Not that bad? Summer remembered the way Gertrude Beesley glared at her in the dressing room before the show.

Carl bent down to whisper with Aunt Clara, and Summer paid a lot of attention to the booklet in order to give them privacy. It was a stack of mostly handmade coupons to various local restaurants and attractions. She flipped through quickly, finding one for a coffee shop. She'd been dying for a real cup of coffee since her plane landed. It looked close, but was it worth getting dressed and leaving the comfort of the pool?

———

"So it's settled." Carl stood and took Aunt Clara's hand.

"What's settled?" Summer asked.

"I'm taking you two lovely ladies into town. Lunch...and hopefully dinner...are on me." He said that last part with a longing glance at Aunt Clara, who did not shoot the idea down.

So much for relaxing and secretly looking for the handsome man. "Fine, as long as coffee's on the menu."

"Oh, definitely. The best coffee this side of Seattle."

"Great. I'm in."

"Perfect. I have a few people I'd like to introduce you to. Maybe tear into that little coupon book of yours."

The way things were looking, they had exactly two days to burn through this coupon book before she had to hit the road. Might as well start now. She gave the book back to Carl. "We're all yours."

His eyes shined at that, and he couldn't resist the quick glance in Aunt Clara's direction. "Also, I was thinking." Carl took Aunt Clara's arm and began to lead them through the pool house and past the Rec Center. "Since my son, Henry, isn't here to sweep you off your feet, I have someone else to introduce you to. He's a good boy. Came here to care for his ailing mother and-"

"I'm fine staying *on* my feet, thank you," Summer said, following close behind the two obvious lovebirds.

"Come on, help an old man out here, kid." Carl smiled back over his shoulder at Summer. "If I can dangle a handsome carrot in front of you to keep you here long enough, I might be able to score a dance with your lovely aunt at the Fall Ball."

"Did you just call me a horse?"

Carl and Aunt Clara burst with laughter, but it was drowned out by another sound. A shrill scream echoed through the whole campground just as they exited the pool house.

Summer stopped dead in her tracks. "What was that?"

"I don't know," Carl said as he dropped Aunt Clara's hand and ran...toward the scream.

Summer didn't have time to think before Aunt Clara took off after him. Her only option was to follow.

When they reached the screams, for there were several more in the span of seconds it took to run across the yard, Summer found herself standing in the back doorway of the Rec Center. The room looked so different now in the light of day. The tables where she'd worked so hard on Aunt Clara's hair were all folded against the wall now. Several chairs were stacked high beside them. All the mirrors were gone. Half the room was swept, while the other half was still strewn with hair clips, spray bottles, and snippets of wayward strands that must not have obeyed last night.

And against the far wall, partially obscured by a tall counter, was a dead body.

5

Summer stumbled back, trying to pull Aunt Clara with her. But her aunt still had ahold of Carl's hand. Summer had never seen a dead body before. Never seen the pallid color of someone's skin after...

No!

She shook her head and refused to think about it. Refused to look. Instead, she eyed the crowd that was still growing, still gathering around this poor woman.

When she began hearing the whispers, she got even more terrified.

"Wasn't she at the new girl's table?"

"Isn't that their hair dryer?"

"Did you see them after the contest? I sure didn't."

All it took was another glance around the room to confirm her suspicion. All eyes were on her and Aunt Clara.

"Um," she said, tugging at Aunt Clara's free hand. "I think we need to go."

"What? Why? We need to help." Then, Aunt Clara must have also felt the eyes boring holes into her because she stood and pulled her hand away from Carl, placing it over her heart. "You can't think I..."

Carl stepped back, covering both of them with his own body. "Has anyone called the Sheriff?"

"He's on the way," a young woman said from the back.

Summer looked toward the voice and saw the back of a man's head leaving the room. She wasn't sure but she thought it was the handsome man from the contest.

"I can't believe it."

"Who would do such a thing?"

"Someone with a grudge."

The last one sent more distrustful glances at Aunt Clara.

Summer leaned over to whisper in her aunt's ear. "Why are they looking at you? What don't I know?"

Aunt Clara sank backward against Summer's chest and heaved a sigh. "That's Marsha Peterson. The current owner of the campground."

Summer waited. She'd heard some bad things about Marsha but nothing that would suggest her Aunt Clara would be suspected of murdering her.

"Everyone's so upset about it and...you know me. I can't keep my mouth shut."

"What did you do?"

"We exchanged words the day before you landed. It got pretty heated."

"Isn't she the one who showed us to our work stations last night? She seemed fine. I mean, there wasn't any animosity between you...certainly not like with the Beesley Twins." Summer didn't think they were actually twins, but their attitudes were.

"Yes, she owns-owned the place. I guess her husband does now." Aunt Clara shook her head. "Anyway, some of us had a few choice words for her the last time she was here. It didn't go well."

"And by some, you mean you."

Aunt Clara nodded.

"Oh, this isn't good. We need to get you out-"

"Not so fast!"

Summer grabbed Aunt Clara's arm, but someone else grabbed the other and wouldn't let go. Someone who wasn't Carl. A tall, burly man had Aunt Clara and wasn't letting go. His meaty hand took up most of Aunt Clara's upper arm, and the other was pointing at the body.

"Is that your blow dryer or not?"

Aunt Clara was shaking her head and opened her mouth, but Summer pushed in front of her. "She doesn't have to answer to you. Who do you think you are?"

They struggled for control of Aunt Clara, and the large man won.

"I'm her husband!" The rage coming off the man had everyone stepping back, except for Aunt Clara, who was trapped in his grasp.

A hush fell over the crowd, followed by hushed chatter.

"Frank." It was Carl's voice breaking through the whispers. He moved toward the man like a boxer in a ring. "Frank, let the nice woman go. I can assure she had nothing to do with this."

Frank? That didn't sound right to Summer, but she couldn't figure out why.

"Is that your blow dryer?" Frank didn't so much as loosen his grip on Aunt Clara.

"It's mine," Summer said, defiantly, craning her neck to be face to face with the giant.

"No," Aunt Clara corrected, softly. "It's not hers. We borrowed it for the contest but I will not say who from, not with this behavior." For someone with no children, she sure had mastered the disappointed parent tone, especially since Frank looked to be only ten years younger than her. She tugged at her arm, but it didn't budge.

The man kept hold of Aunt Clara's arm but moved toward Summer and reached for her. Aunt Clara jerked hard in the other direction, giving Summer time to run.

Only there was nowhere *to* run. The whole crowd of people had closed in on them.

"That's enough!"

Everyone turned to see another large, muscular man in an overly tight sheriff uniform.

———

"What's all this?" The Sheriff lumbered toward them, taking off his sunglasses like a movie star.

Carl was the only one brave enough to speak. "Thank God, Brady. These people have gone mad."

Sheriff Brady scanned the room, his gaze landing on Summer, Aunt Clara, and the giant squeezing the life out of Aunt Clara's arm. "Frank, what are you doing here?"

Frank shook Aunt Clara and pointed a thick finger at Summer. "They killed her, Ronnie. They killed Marsha!"

"We did no such thing!" Aunt Clara's tone had changed to one of fury. "We came in here *after* hearing the scream. Just like every one of you!" She pointed her own thin finger at the crowd.

"People saw you fighting with her the other day. And now your blow dryer is..." Frank put a hand in front of his neck, unable to say the words.

Summer forced herself to look once more, made her eyes roam up the poor dead woman's body. The cord of a blow dryer was wrapped around her neck. And sticking out from the end of it was their contestant number, 31.

"Frank," Sheriff Brady said again, "Why are *you* here?"

"I'm keeping these two from running." He gave Aunt Clara another shake.

"No." Sheriff Brady closed the distance between them and placed his hand atop Frank's, slowly peeling back his massive fingers until Aunt Clara's arm was finally free. "Why are you in town?"

Summer gasped. Whether at her aunt's escape or the Sheriff's words, she didn't know. Why wasn't the dead woman's husband supposed to be in town?

"Jacobson," Sheriff Brady said, turning to Carl, "why don't you take—" He glanced at Aunt Clara and Summer—"I'm sorry. What are your names?" They told him and he continued, "Why don't you take Ms. Snow and Ms. Newberg over to Concessions and get them something to drink while Frank and I have a chat?"

Carl nodded, taking both their hands.

"As for the rest of you..." Sheriff Brady raised his hands to the crowd and moved in front of the body. "Show's over."

Summer let Carl lead them to a small concession stand across from the Rec Center. It looked like a log cabin, which she supposed was fitting. But after the events that just unfolded, she already felt too much like she was living in an old Western movie. She wanted...she wasn't sure what she wanted, but it wasn't going to come from a log cabin.

Carl sat them both at a picnic table and went to the front window of the cabin. When he returned a few minutes later with drinks and a basket of fries, they were still silently staring into nothing.

"Here, eat this. Get some salt into you. It'll help."

Neither argued as they mindlessly picked at the fries.

People milled about, some likely oblivious to the drama unfolding mere feet from them, laughing and playing in line as they waited for their corn dogs and nachos. Others, after being dismissed by the Sheriff, still walked slowly back and forth whispering. Summer knew they were talking about her and Aunt Clara, but she didn't have the mental space to worry about them.

"Why isn't he supposed to be here?" Summer asked after a few minutes, the thought she'd been stuck on tumbling out of her mouth.

"Frank?"

"Yeah, if he's her husband, why isn't he supposed to be in town?"

"Ex husband."

Summer blinked away the haze that had been clouding her mind. "Her ex husband was in town, when she turned up dead, and everyone thinks *we* did it?"

Carl shook his head. "Frank would never-"

"*We* would never!"

"No! No, of course not! It's just...Frank is a nice guy. I don't know why he's back, but it couldn't have anything to do with...that."

"Well, someone did *that* and now everyone seems to think it was us." Summer glared at the people walking by with their eyes glued to her and Aunt Clara, hands covering their mouths as if she didn't already know what they were saying.

"Not us," Aunt Clara said, holding a fry up to her mouth but not eating. "Me. They think I..." Her voice trailed off and the fry hung in the air.

"That's just absurd. Because you had words with her? If half the stuff I've heard so far about her shady business dealings with that councilman is true, I'm sure the whole town has a problem with her."

"The whole town didn't have their blow dryer wrapped around her neck."

6

Summer was about to argue that it wasn't her blow dryer. They'd borrowed it. But Sheriff Brady stood before them, holding a small notebook.

"Ladies," he said, not unkindly.

Carl looked around and then asked, "Where's Frank?"

Sheriff Brady jutted his pen over his shoulder. "In the car." When Summer and Aunt Clara both gasped, he added, "Just waiting for me. We're gonna go down to the station and take a formal statement. He's got to get back home soon. But for now, I'd like to ask you ladies a couple of questions."

Summer hated the way he said 'ladies' but wasn't about to point that out. "What do you need to know? We'd also like to get home soon."

"For starters, did you see anything suspicious?"

Summer let out a breath. That was a perfectly normal question to ask a witness, not a suspect. "I saw a man..." She turned to Aunt Clara. "You know that really handsome guy who was getting his hair done next to us? I only saw the back of his head, but he was leaving just as the crowd started gathering."

Sheriff Brady made a note. "Very handsome man. Got it. Do either of you know who that was?" He looked at Carl when he said it.

"Sorry, I wasn't back there when they were working on Clara's hair. I didn't see the other contestants."

Aunt Clara only shook her head.

"And where did you get the blow dryer?"

Summer debated what to say. She didn't want to get anyone in trouble, but she really wanted to get Aunt Clara *out* of trouble. But it was Aunt Clara who spoke for both of them. "Someone who isn't a murderer, either. She wasn't even here when Marsha was killed."

Sheriff Brady wrote something in his notebook. "How do you know?"

"Because she wasn't here."

"But how do you know she wasn't here when the murder took place? Do you know when that was? Exactly?" Sheriff Brady's eyebrows shot up.

Carl put out a hand before Summer could say or do something to get them in more trouble than they were already in. "Come on, now. Let's just calm down. Sheriff, I can vouch for Clara and her niece. *And...*" He emphasized that last word and paused for effect. "Considering Summer here won the contest, and Clara was her model, I can assure you they were way too busy to be murdering anyone. Plus, if you think about it, that would explain her blow dryer being at the scene."

At the scene. Summer didn't like the sound of that either.

"Carl, are you suggesting someone killed Marsha with Ms. Newberg's *friend's* blow dryer because they won a hair contest?"

"I'm not suggesting anything. All I'm saying is it wasn't them. And you and I both know murders have been committed for much less. People are crazy."

"What about jealousy?" Summer asked.

Sheriff Brady scribbled on his notepad again. "What kind?"

"Well, the oldest kind in the book. Why wasn't Frank supposed to be in town? Her ex-husband? And didn't someone say she had a hot new—very young—third husband?"

Sheriff Brady shook his head. "I'm taking Frank down to the station after this, and I'll find out exactly what's going on with that. But he's not the type to...he loved Marsha."

"And my aunt's not the type, either."

A voice came over the Sheriff's radio, a staticky female saying that the medical examiner needed him at the entrance gate.

"Alright, we'll finish this later. How about you follow me to the station and..."

"How about," Carl said, moving closer to Sheriff Brady to whisper. "How about I take these lovely ladies out for ice cream like we'd planned? I'm sure they could use a break after what they've just gone through."

"Carl, come on. You know I can't."

Food was the last thing on Summer's mind, but she desperately needed to get out of here. "Please? I've only got two more days in town and I haven't been able to see the sights. I promise we'll come to the station tomorrow."

"This is highly—Don't go anywhere. You need to make other arrangements. Until this is solved, nobody's leaving town." Sheriff Brady leveled a stern look at Summer, then Aunt Clara. "Nobody."

Summer started to protest but Carl placed a hand on her arm. "Of course. I'll take custody and responsibility for both of them."

Sheriff Brady hesitated, not wanting to give in, until his mind was made up by the radio crackling again. "Fine. But stick together. They're your responsibility, Jacobson."

The Sheriff walked away, answering the woman on his radio.

"Now," Carl said, slapping his hands against his thighs. "Who's up for some ice cream?"

Summer and Aunt Clara exchanged disgusted looks.

"Alright, alright. No ice cream. But we're still going to town. I promised you some coffee, right? I know you need that!"

As much as Summer was torn between hiding in Aunt Clara's RV and starting the thing up and getting the heck out of town, she could never turn down a good cup of coffee. "OK. Coffee it is."

Summer took Aunt Clara's hand and led her through the gawking crowd, past the police car where Frank was sitting with his head in his hands. She didn't look long enough to tell if he was crying. She'd had enough trauma for one day.

"Did you work with Sheriff Brady?" Summer asked when they finally reached Carl's car.

"Yeah, he was just coming up the ranks when I was heading out to pasture. He's a good guy. Got his priorities straight. He's fair and thorough, but..."

"But what?"

"Poor guy's in over his head with something like this."

"A murder?" It seemed to Summer like that was exactly what the Sheriff's job was supposed to be.

"Not just murder. The murder of a prominent—though allegedly shady—businesswoman in the middle of a packed location with hundreds of potential witnesses and contaminants." Carl opened the front passenger door and helped Aunt Clara in. Then he opened the back for Summer.

Summer didn't like the sound of that as she allowed him to hold the door for her. Clearly her aunt was the prime suspect, despite the obvious love triangle brewing. And if the Sheriff was in over his head, where did that leave them?

All of a sudden, her stomach soured at the thought of even a cup of coffee, which was beginning to feel like their last meal.

———

They spent the first couple hours of their trip to town wandering aimlessly. Summer figured that was Carl's way of letting them work through what had happened on their own. He never pressured them to go into any stores or talk about anything. He simply walked beside or behind them, keeping to himself.

Until they came to the main strip in the heart of town.

"Here we are!" Carl stopped abruptly in front of a small coffee shop.

The awning was red with a blue stripe down the center, not exactly fitting with the beach cottage theme of the rest of the town, but close enough that it still looked like it belonged. Above the awning was a giant coffee cup with the name "Spring in Your Step" rising out of the smoke tendrils. The large window was covered in Polaroid pictures of happy customers, and Summer instantly knew she was going to love the place.

"I promised you the best ice cream in town and here it is."

Aunt Clara hesitated, clearly looking at the giant coffee cup sign, but Summer walked right in.

And froze.

Behind the counter was the most handsome man she'd ever seen. He had thick, wavy brown hair and eyes to match. His black t-shirt didn't do much to hide the tan muscular arms working an industrial coffee grinder.

Carl breezed past her. "Evan! How's Daisy? Tell her I said congrats on second place in the Crazy Hair Contest."

Summer blinked, still not budging. This was the handsome man she saw at the contest. Which meant she beat out his poor daughter for first place. Yet another reason to regret entering.

"This is Summer and her aunt Clara. They're here to get some of your world famous ice cream." Carl stepped aside, leaving Summer no choice but to move.

She put out her hand to greet him. "Hi, nice to meet you. I didn't recognize you without all those clips in your hair."

Evan took her hand and smiled. "I would recognize you anywhere."

Summer frowned, trying to read his expression. Clearly he'd been at the campground earlier, when the body was discovered. And he had to see everyone blaming them for the woman's death. Did they now have a target on their backs? Well, that was fine because *he* was the one leaving the scene, not her. She was glad she told the Sheriff about it, too. And now she had a name and place of business to put with the face—or the back of the head.

She realized she was still shaking his hand and pulled away. What was she doing? She couldn't identify someone by the back of their head. Could she? Without looking too suspicious, she tried, but he'd already turned his attention to Aunt Clara and Carl.

When she looked back at them, she caught some sort of knowing look being exchanged. One she couldn't read.

"Three of your largest coffee floats, please. Mocha for me. How about you?" Carl smiled at Aunt Clara.

"Caramel."

Everyone turned to Summer. "Caramel."

"Perfect," Evan said and held out his hand again.

Summer reached to shake it. Evan laughed, but still took her hand. Then, when the laugh turned to just a smile, after a long uncomfortable thirty seconds, he said, "I assume you're turning in your coupon."

Summer gasped and jerked her hand from him, then dug the coupon book out of her pocket and tore out the one for his shop. She dropped it in the same hand she'd been foolishly holding.

"Great! They'll be right up!" Thankfully, Evan spun on his heels and went about making their floats before he could see the bright red flush of her cheeks.

She didn't dare turn back toward Aunt Clara and Carl yet. Instead, she took an inordinate amount of time picking the perfect size straws and the correct number of napkins for their table.

When she finally reached the table they'd chosen, she caught them exchanging yet another subtext filled glance.

"What?"

Aunt Clara smirked and opened her mouth to say something, but was distracted by movement beside them.

Coming through the front door was Mrs. Beesley. She was alone this time but no less catty when she saw them all staring. Her response was a cold, hard glare at each one of them individually before sauntering up to the counter.

Summer was half trying to eavesdrop on her, which turned out to be unnecessary. In a loud tone, Mrs. Beesley said, "They'll let just about anyone in here."

In an equally loud manner, Evan replied, "I know, right? Sheriff Brady said I wasn't allowed to refuse you service anymore, so here we are. What'll I get you?"

Summer nearly choked on the laugh that erupted from her chest.

7

S ummer was going stir crazy, cooped up in the RV. She felt like a kid who'd been grounded all summer break. Watching the other kids run past the window, playing and laughing.

It had been two days since Marsha Peterson's body was discovered and nothing had happened. Nothing except for leers and whispers every time they dared venture outside. So they stopped venturing and settled into a torturous routine of pacing the RV and not watching whatever was on the small TV.

Aunt Clara wasn't doing much better. Summer had never seen her so...broken. She hadn't even bothered to put her curlers in the night before and now her hair just fell limply over her shoulders. Summers' fingers itched to braid it or give her a cute updo, but she didn't think either of them could handle the memories it would trigger.

"I'm sorry I got you into this mess," Aunt Clara said after her third trip to open the tiny refrigerator and close it without getting anything.

"What? No. Don't be sorry. You had no way of knowing someone would...*die*." She whispered the last part, unable to bring herself to say the word out loud.

"I knew my mouth would get me in trouble one day."

Summer had to laugh at that. "Yeah, I kinda knew that, too. But we can get you out of this. If the cops aren't gonna do it. Then we will."

Aunt Clara looked as if she would argue, but she straightened her back and headed for the fridge again. This time, she reached up to the freezer and pulled out their leftover coffee floats. "Brain fuel."

Summer clapped her hands and shoved everything to one side of the small dining table. "Of course!"

After setting the floats down—Carl was right about them being the best thing she'd ever tasted—Aunt Clara started searching the cabinets in the sitting area.

"What are you doing?"

"We need something to write on." She pulled out an old magazine, checking the edges for white space.

"Aunt Clara..." Summer dragged the words out like she was talking to a senile old woman. Then she waved her phone in the air. "What year is it?"

They both laughed and Aunt Clara sat down across from Summer. "Alright, what do we know so far?"

Summer swiped her screen to get to her notes app and noticed a text from Vanessa that read, '*You in prison yet?*'

She rolled her eyes and set back a, '*Yep!*' Though, the mention of prison struck a fear in her that she'd rather not think about right now. Considering the trouble that was sure to follow her from Georgia, the last thing she needed right now was another reason to be locked up.

She'd filled her best friend in on the drama and now had to field constant questions and check-ins from across the globe. As of last night, she was pretty sure Vanessa was now in Bali. The life of an influencer must be exhausting.

Summer opened the notes app and started typing as she spoke, "Suspects. Definitely the ex husband, right? And the new one?"

"Yeah, I mean, why was Frank in town? It sounded like Sheriff Brady didn't like that."

Summer nodded. "Yeah, but also what if he was here to protect her from the new husband? What was his name? Mario?"

Aunt Clara nodded and took her time before speaking again. "Could be someone she works with. Or did some shady dealings with."

"Like that councilman? How is he still involved in all the real estate stuff if he's a member of government now?"

"We might be in California, but this is still a very small town. Those things happen. But it's definitely a conflict of interest."

Summer wrote Drew Harding's name down, then hesitated. "I don't know how I feel about this, but..."

"But what?" Aunt Clara took a huge bite of her frozen coffee float and seemed to be doing her best to hide a brain freeze.

"Evan, from the coffee shop."

Aunt Clara's face twisted into a different type of pained expression, but she still wasn't able to speak.

Summer continued. "The hot guy I told the Sheriff about, the one who left right when the body was found...I have a bad feeling that it was him."

Aunt Clara tapped the back of Summer's phone, and Summer obeyed by typing his name on the list.

"I don't like it, but fair is fair."

Aunt Clara chose that moment to be over her brain freeze and ask, "Because he's hot?"

Summer gasped. "Aunt Clara!" She put a hand to her chest like clutching nonexistent pearls. "Yes," she admitted, sheepishly.

A smirk curled one side of Aunt Clara's lips. "If I was thirty years younger..."

"Hey! You've got a man!" Plus, this guy's on the suspect list, she didn't have the heart to say. Or the fact that he was at the contest with a child, which meant a wife was also somewhere close by.

The smirk disappeared and Aunt Clara began chewing on her lip.

"What?" Summer asked, fingers ready to start typing again.

"What if the murder wasn't about Marsha, but about framing me for killing someone? Anyone."

"And who would do that?"

Summer didn't like her first thought, which went right to Mr. DeVilla. But she shook her head. There was no way he found her this fast and already had time to rack up another body.

Besides, she knew what Aunt Clara was thinking before she had a chance to say, "Ramona."

"Do you really think she'd..."

A knock on the door made both women jump. Aunt Clara's spoon fell from her hand and clanged on the table.

Summer didn't know what Aunt Clara was thinking, but she was sure thinking her aunt's love triangle rival was here to finish the job. She bolted for the door, grabbing a spatula on the way. "Who is it?"

A stern male voice said through the door, "Sheriff Brady. It's time we had that talk."

Somehow, this felt worse than facing a possibly murderous old lady.

———

The Sheriff's office didn't smell the way Summer had expected. Though she had nothing to go on besides TV and movies, she'd always assumed they smelled like a locker room. This one smelled like the beach. It went a long way toward settling her nerves as she and Aunt Clara followed Sheriff Brady through the winding hallway.

"You're in here," he said, pointing between Aunt Clara and a thick metal door with a shaded window.

"Don't say a word," Summer whispered. "Ask for a lawyer and zip it."

Aunt Clara patted her hand before stepping into the room. "I have nothing to hide."

When the door thudded shut with a heavy metallic noise, Summer glared at Sheriff Brady. "I'll have your badge if anything happens to her."

"You heard her," he said, with a smile Summer couldn't read other than to think it looked grim. "She has nothing to hide. And I'm sure neither do you." He pointed to a room right across the hall with a matching scary door.

"Nothing to hide and nothing to say that will help you. Because...we...weren't...there."

"That's what everyone's been saying. Now, can you please have a seat?"

Summer took the metal folding chair and waited for Sheriff Brady to settle his massive frame into the nice office chair across from her. "Great, so everyone already told you we weren't there? How can I help, then?"

Sheriff Brady clicked his pen. "No, everyone said *they* weren't there. I just have to weed through all the truths to find the one lie."

Summer groaned. "Well, it's not us."

The Sheriff only nodded. "Alright then, what did you do after you won the hair contest?"

With a shrug, Summer told him about their night. "We went back to the RV. I knew it would take a long time to get all that paint and spray out of my aunt's hair. And..."

Sheriff Brady waited a few seconds before prompting, "And?"

"And the vibe was off. It was clear some of the other contestants didn't like that we won."

"Like who?"

"Look, I don't think they killed that poor woman over jealousy. And I don't want to just throw names out there. There was tension between my aunt and someone...*else*... not the victim. We went back to her RV and did a puzzle."

"What kind of puzzle?"

"Cats. What other kind of puzzle would you expect from a sixty-three-year-old woman?"

"And this handsome man you saw? Can you describe him a little better, please?" Sheriff Brady's pen hovered over his little notepad.

Summer hesitated. Now, in the light of day, and after meeting Evan, she wasn't really sure what she saw that morning. "Dark brown, wavy hair, not quite to the shoulders."

Sheriff Brady stared at her for a moment. "So dark brown wavy hair is handsome? That's all you got?"

Summer squirmed in the uncomfortable metal chair. "I saw the back of his head, walking out the door and assumed it was the man who had been in the contest. The hair looked the same."

"And that was handsome?"

"Is this pertinent to your murder investigation?"

Sheriff Brady only stared at her, waiting.

"The man had been handsome, and when I saw the brown hair, I thought it was him. But considering there was also a dead body in the room, my attention was elsewhere. I can't be sure now if it was him or not." She leveled him with a look that dared him to continue down that line of questioning.

"Well then, I think we have our killer." Summer nearly gasped before Sheriff Brady grinned. "I'll write up an arrest warrant for every handsome man in Spring Harbor, if you'd be so kind as to ride around with me and point them out."

Instead of a gasp, Summer let out an annoyed groan and narrowed her eyes at the sheriff.

"Wait here." Sheriff Brady stood up and walked out of the room. A couple minutes later, he returned and gestured for her to get up. "You're free to go, for now. Just don't go too far."

"What about my aunt?"

He stepped aside, and Summer saw her Aunt Clara coming out of the other room. She went to her aunt and wrapped her in a bear hug. "Are you all right?"

Before Aunt Clara could answer, a beautiful young woman and gorgeous man stood at the end of the hallway. Both had murderous looks in their eyes, which were trained directly on Aunt Clara.

Summer assumed they were Marsha Peterson's children until she caught the dark tan skin and jet black curls of the young man. Her much younger third husband. Alex had been right, they were practically the same age.

Was that motive enough for murder?

As they passed the couple, Summer watched the woman intently. Jennifer, she remembered, was the daughter's name. She was dressed in matching black silk pants and blouse. Her hair was half up, which would look normal on any other woman, but was a clear indication that she was disheveled. As she lifted her hand to dab her nose with a crumpled tissue, several bracelets jangled on her wrist, and the harsh sheriff's office lighting glinted off a handful of rings.

As if that weren't bad enough, when they were headed toward the door to make their escape, she saw Alex standing at the front desk with tear stains running down her cheek. Summer tried to make eye contact, but it was clear that Alex was trying hard not to look at her.

"Come on," Aunt Clara said, grabbing Summer's hand and pulling her toward the door.

On the other side were the Beesley twins. Both glared down at Aunt Clara, and not just because they were a head taller than her. In body language alone, Summer knew it was her turn to grab her aunt's arm and drag her away before another murder happened.

8

"Well that sucked."

Summer finally let out the gasp that had been trying to escape. "Aunt Clara!"

"Well it did." Aunt Clara moved to Summer's other side, the side closest to the road, as they walked down the street. So Summer went around her aunt so she would be closest to the road. They talked and danced around each other this way the whole walk back.

They stopped briefly outside the coffee shop, but it was closed up already. Summer pulled out her phone and saw that it was only 4 PM. She also saw another text from Vanessa.

'Your post has been blowing up! You really need to get back on your Insta and post some tutorials'

She swiped the message away. The last thing she needed right now was to be all over social media. She shouldn't have allowed Vanessa to post that hairstyle.

"Is this going to make things harder on you? With all the other stuff going on…" Aunt Clara waved her hand in the general direction of where Summer assumed Georgia would be.

No, Summer tried not to groan, but a small sound came out anyway. Yes, this mess would make that one a lot worse. It was also all the more reason she shouldn't be plastered on socials right now. She thought about asking Vanessa to take the post down, but something stopped her. She hoped it wasn't her ego.

"I'm sure it'll be fine," she lied.

Summer didn't want to think about anything from back home right now. She came to California for a reason. Escape. And it seemed she ran right into another terrible situation. She should have known better. Known you can't escape your problems, even by running halfway across the country.

"So who do you think did it?" She needed to change the subject.

"Well, my money was on Frank at first. Ex-husband showing up out of the blue right when she turns up dead? Seemed open and shut to me."

"Seemed?"

Aunt Clara stopped walking. "Yeah, now I'm not so sure. From the questions they were asking me, I think they suspect the new husband."

"What kind of questions?" She thought back to her conversation with Sheriff Brady, and it certainly sounded like there was a theme.

"Mostly about the handsome man you saw leaving. I think they wanted me to tell them it was Mario, but I said I didn't see him."

"You know, it felt like that's where he was trying to steer me also. But the more I think about it, the less sure I am."

Aunt Clara only nodded and started walking again, but the expression on her face spoke volumes.

"What?" Summer chased after her.

"Nothing...just that Evan is rather handsome, isn't he?"

"Ugh, Aunt Clara!"

"What? He is. And you two looked so cute together."

"You do remember he was getting his hair done by his daughter, right? And I'm sure his *wife* was waiting in the audience to cheer them on. And that they look even cuter together."

They walked in silence that was only uncomfortable for her. When she saw the big neon "Wheels Up!" sign, Summer let herself relax.

Though, what she saw after she entered the RV park set tension back in her shoulders. The handsome man and wife in question were sitting at a picnic table with two coffee cups from his shop. Their cute little girl was beside him, giving him a big side-hug with one arm while devouring a chocolate muffin.

When he caught her staring, she quickly lowered her head and nudged Aunt Clara to move faster.

Was there a reason he—they—would want Mrs. Peterson dead? Why ruin a beautiful family by committing murder? If Evan really was the killer, it must have been to protect his wife and daughter. But what could drive a man to do that?

"Do you know what kind of shady deals she was doing?" Summer asked, voicing only the last part of her train of thought.

Aunt Clara didn't skip a beat. "Not really, but I'm sure we know someone who does."

That was when Summer finally looked up to see they weren't at Aunt Clara's RV, where she could go in and take a nice, hot shower and wash the day off of her. No, they were standing at Carl's door and Aunt Clara was knocking.

"Ladies!" Carl's booming voice echoed through his tiny camper and Summer was sure all the neighbors heard. "To what do I owe this pleasure?"

Despite not feeling social, she quickly darted inside. The faster they got through this, the faster she and her aunt could get out of Dodge.

Aunt Clara sat on one side of the tiny table and Carl started to climb into the other side before catching himself and offering the seat to Summer. They looked so natural. She couldn't help but wonder how much time they'd spent together just like this.

She shook her head and Carl took the seat. Even after that walk back from town, Summer still had way too much nervous energy to burn. She started pacing the cramped room, half thinking and half muttering under her breath.

She felt like a caged animal. She never had wanderlust like Aunt Clara, but she'd inherited enough of it that being told she can't leave town made it the number one thing she wanted to do. It didn't matter that she had nowhere to go.

She certainly couldn't go back to Atlanta. Not until that ordeal was over. Her parents were in Wyoming. A nice, quiet retirement community where everyone raved about the 'dry heat.' She couldn't very well disturb their peace, or bring all her drama to their doorstep. And as much as she loved Vanessa, the last thing she wanted was to tag along all over the world, though it had been offered many times. Long before...what happened in Atlanta.

And now, if they didn't figure out this whole murder thing, her poor Aunt Clara would have the same dark cloud hanging over her wherever she went. She couldn't allow that.

"Care to enlighten us on what's going through that pretty little head of yours?" Carl's gruff voice broke her pity spiral. The words coming from anyone but him would have irked her, but somehow they seemed endearing the way he said them.

She stopped pacing and stood at the edge of the table. "I don't think the cops are any closer to figuring this case out. The questions Sheriff Brady asked were too generic. And we're still not allowed to leave town. My flight is coming up. Aunt Clara has her ski trip. It..It's..." Summer finally let out a breath.

Carl nodded. "Yes, it is. Like I said, Ronnie's in over his head. But I've been thinking about the case myself. I say we start where I always start and see what we can figure out together."

"And where's that?"

"The victim. Who she was. Who she knew. Who would want her dead."

Summer threw up her arms. "We don't know anything about her besides what all of y'all told us. She was crooked. She traded in husbands for younger models." Summer stopped. "That right there is enough to get you killed. Jealousy. And not over something as trivial as a hair styling contest."

Aunt Clara shook her head. "No, I don't think it was over the contest, regardless. The people pointing fingers at me are saying I threatened her about selling this place." She waved her hand around. "Which...I did. Sort of. I didn't threaten her, really. But I said she'd be sorry."

Summer raised one eyebrow.

"Not like that. I meant her conscience would eat at her. Selling something out from under this community, something they all love so much that it's usually so full of locals there's hardly ever space for travelers."

"What about the ex-husband?"

"No," Carl said. "I know it looks bad, but there has to be an explanation. Frank just isn't the type of person to do such a thing. He still loved Marsha to..."

"Death?" Summer finished for him when he didn't.

"You know what I mean." Carl ran a hand over his face. "He was devastated when Marsha asked for the divorce. He'd been in Jennie's life since she was three. He still loved them both, dearly."

"You're not exactly talking me out of my theory."

"I know the guy. It's not him."

They stared at each other in a stalemate before Aunt Clara broke the spell. "What about the new husband? I'm sure he'd stand to gain a lot of money if she..."

Carl heaved a big sigh. "Maybe, but I'm sure by the time she got to hubby number three, Marsha was a pro at prenups."

The camper was silent for several long minutes until Aunt Clara asked, "So where does that leave us?"

Summer said the only thing she'd been thinking about the whole time. "Back at square one."

9

"How do you think that went?" Summer asked Aunt Clara after coming out of her super hot shower. Her hair was dripping wet but she wasn't about to go near another blow dryer...even if she had one. She hated wrapping her hair in a towel, but air drying just wasn't an option for her. She'd deal with the frizz tomorrow.

Aunt Clara didn't respond right away, prompting Summer to pay closer attention to her demeanor. She was sitting at the table, palming a mug of coffee but not drinking. Summer was sure it was only there for comfort. Lines she had never noticed before seemed prominent on her aunt's forehead. "I think you should go," was all she said.

"What? No!" Summer let go of the towel, not caring about her hair anymore. "I'm not leaving you to deal with this by yourself." Aunt Clara opened her mouth but Summer shushed her. "And don't you dare say you aren't by yourself because you have Carl."

"I was going to say I'd rather deal with it by myself than have you going through this. I'd rather be locked up already than…"

"I don't care." Summer interrupted, her tone kind but firm. "And besides, I'm here now. Sheriff Macho Man Brady isn't about to let me go anywhere."

That, at least, elicited a smile. "He does look like Macho Man, doesn't he?"

"If he grows his hair out…already got the tan."

They both laughed and a quiet ease settled between them. A few calm minutes went by before Aunt Clara sighed. "Guess I'll be canceling my ski trip. What are you gonna do? Whether you leave now or not, I'd much prefer you going to Wyoming than back to Atlanta. I worry about you."

Summer leaned in. "One, you're not canceling anything. We may have to postpone, but no canceling. And two, if you send me to that retirement village, I'll be so bored I'd probably walk back to Atlanta."

"Well, we can't have that. So what do we do?"

"Are you sure you don't like the Beesley Twins for it?"

Last time Mrs. Beesley came up, right after bumping into them at the station, Aunt Clara had immediately said she didn't suspect them. Now, with more time and worry, she thought longer before speaking. Still, she shook her head in the end. "No. I think Ramona would love to see me disappear so she could have Carl all to herself. But not enough to frame me for murder. And Gertie, I think she just always has that judging look on her face. And honestly, if we're both going to be stuck here for a while, you should talk to her about the salon. You'd love it here—murder charges notwithstanding."

Summer ignored the latter part and asked, "Do you like him?"

Aunt Clara's face was the picture of innocence, except the two red circles blossoming on her cheeks. "He's a nice man."

"Nice enough to come between him and Ramona when you know you're going to leave town again?"

"There was no 'him and Ramona' before I came to town." Her tone made it clear the conversation on that subject was over.

Summer went to the kitchen counter and fixed them peanut butter sandwiches. She needed something to do with her hands.

When she came back to the table, Aunt Clara took her sandwich but didn't touch it. "Seriously, though, what are you going to do after this? You know you can come with me if you want, but that's not the life you want. You need a place you can set up roots." Aunt Clara laughed. "That's why you should work at the salon. Get it? Roots?" When Summer only shook her head slowly at the pun, Aunt Clara added, "I'd hate to see her sell it to someone else and then you regret your decision."

"Sell it? I don't have the money for that! I'd have to sign myself up for a lifetime of indentured servitude before coming up with a down payment."

"I could..."

"No."

Summer wished she had other options, something else to distract her aunt from this silly notion that she could run her own salon. She'd learned the hard way just how much she wasn't a leader. The one time she'd tried, her whole world had blown up in her face.

She could get another dead end job, pushing papers for the next thirty years, if she wanted one. Her old supervisor, Mr. Hubbard, had said he'd give her a glowing recommendation...as long as she ended up somewhere fast. Before word got out.

But even as she entertained the idea, she knew she didn't want that for herself. Not anymore. She just wasn't sure she had the guts to go for what she did want.

"What about the daughter and the husband?" She needed to change the subject again. "It's always the husband, right? And do we even want to think about the daughter? Wasn't she also involved in the real estate deals?"

Aunt Clara shrugged. "I think so, but that could just be gossip. The same as everyone saying, I'm a murderer now. Plus, I just can't picture anyone...doing that...to their mother. The husband, who knows?"

Summer chewed on her lip. "Maybe it's not about money. Those two looked awful close in that hallway. And they would make a much better couple, don't you think? She's beautiful and he's hot..." She trailed off, thinking again about the other hot elephant in the room.

"Spill it."

"Evan," she whispered, but before she could go on, Aunt Clara slapped her hand on the table.

"No!"

This time, the silence wasn't as comfortable. Then, Aunt Clara spoke up, saying, "Maybe we should leave the detecting to the professionals." She got up from the table, leaving her coffee and sandwich behind.

As she listened to her aunt close the thin bedroom door, she vowed she would do no such thing.

———

The next morning, she wasn't feeling as gung-ho as the night before. She wanted to help Aunt Clara, but honestly had no idea where to start. The only thing she could think of was to do something that would make her aunt happy. So she borrowed the punch buggy and drove into town.

The streets were still full, some obviously tourists with their white zinc noses and safari hats. Mostly, though, it was the normal hustle and bustle of a regular city, only a bit slower than she was used to. Atlanta was a lot more like the Big Apple than people thought.

Even just thinking of back home made her shiver. She wondered if she'd ever be able to look fondly upon her time there without the cloud of Stefan DeVilla hanging over her head.

Another shiver, followed by a near retch. She pulled the car into a parking spot halfway between both her targets and fed her card into the meter. At least this part felt familiar.

The bell hanging over the door tinkled and all heads turned toward her. Two women were at the wash station and two more in the chairs. There was only one stylist that Summer could see, and she looked to be frazzled already.

"Good morning, normally we take walk-ins but we're short staffed today. It's gonna be..."

"Ms. Snow," came a slow, deep drawl that made Summer wonder if Mrs. Beesley used to be a smoker. "May I help you?"

"I think I'm the one who can help you." She wasn't sure why she said it, but the words were out of her mouth before she could stop them.

"And how's that?"

"You saw my work the other night. You're short a person. Let me show you what I can do and..."

"Yes, I've seen your handiwork, Ms. Snow." By her tone, Summer knew she didn't mean Aunt Clara's hair. Her blood boiled, but she kept quiet. "My clients don't require... whatever it is that you did to your aunt. This is a simple, traditional salon, with a very loyal customer base. I'd like to keep it that way."

Summer took in her surroundings. Yes, with its 80s hair posters plastered over faded yellow walls, this whole space was like something out of a John Hughes movie. "Of course. If you're uncomfortable with me cutting, I can work the wash station." She didn't have her supplies on her anyway. The last thing she'd expected to do on this trip was get a job at a hair salon. Well, the second last. Being accused of and trying to solve a murder definitely took the top spot.

Mrs. Beesley looked her up and down, giant beehive nodding, before finally saying, "Alright. Today only. Start at Shampoo and we'll see how it goes."

Summer didn't answer. Instead she ran to the back and grabbed an apron, then proceeded to shampoo, condition, and massage the two women waiting patiently at the wash station. More women filed in and the ordered chaos of the shop settled into a manageable rhythm.

Sometime after lunch, Summer took an older woman with damaged hair over to the stylist, Charlene. When she heard them discussing the cut she wanted, she hesitated. It wasn't her business to interfere, but if the woman got the style she was asking for, Summer knew she'd leave disappointed.

"What is it?" The woman watched her in the mirror, obviously catching her nervous expression.

Summer glanced between Charlene and the customer. "Um, I think you might be disappointed with the way that cut falls once it's washed. Given the damage we discussed earlier...it won't look like that picture."

Charlene took a step back. She didn't look upset, but Summer tread lightly anyway. "I could...show you how to make something similar work."

The customer stared at the picture, then held it up to try visualizing it on her own head. "What do you suggest?"

Summer moved to the other side of the chair and began explaining. You see how the damage on your hair is right here?" She ran her finger around the woman's head along a line that clearly indicated a home coloring incident gone bad. "It's in the exact wrong spot for that style. The best way to get around it is to add an extra layer here first." She indicated a spot half an inch higher than the damage. "It will give a better silhouette and hold up much longer after several washes. Then, on your next cut, you can probably get the style in the picture because the damage will be grown out."

The three of them stood there for a moment, Summer's hands still holding the woman's hair in different places. She pulled and tucked, trying to give the illusion of what the final outcome would be.

The woman smiled. "Let's do that, then. Thank you."

Summer smiled back and dropped the woman's hair. As she was walking away, she caught Mrs. Beesley staring at her from the back room.

She went over for her reprimand. "Sorry," she whispered, "it wasn't going to end well. I shouldn't have overstepped."

"Do you know who that woman is?" Mrs. Beesley always sounded annoyed, and Summer couldn't tell if she was more or less angry with her than what's become their usual.

"No, I'm sorry. I..."

"That's Margaret Edwin." When the name didn't ring a bell for Summer, Mrs. Beesley continued. "Mayor Edwin's wife. And you just told her she had damaged hair."

"Well, she does. But she won't soon."

Mrs. Beesley stiffened. "She's been coming to my salon for decades and none of my girls have ever dared to tell her no."

Summer didn't apologize this time.

"I'm assuming you didn't come here to ask for a job as my wash girl. So what do you want?"

"No, but my aunt told me..." Summer leaned in and whispered. "She told me you might be selling the salon and I just wanted to open up a conversation."

"I thought you were only passing through like your..." Mrs. Beesley caught herself. "What changed?"

What had changed?

The town was lovely, a far cry from where she grew up and where her whole world had just blown up. If this whole murder thing didn't fix itself soon, she might not be allowed to leave. But she couldn't tell Mrs. Beesley that.

Before she finished thinking through her answer, the truth slipped out. "I want to take a chance on myself for once."

Mrs. Beesley studied her for a long time. "Well, mum's the word on selling the place. My children want that, not me. But if the price is right, I could be persuaded. I'll check with Mrs. West and Mr. Harding about valuations...If they're working yet, considering..."

"Considering?"

"Considering your aunt is being accused of their mother's murder."

10

After Summer assured Mrs. Beesley that her aunt had nothing to do with Marsha Peterson's death, she knew she couldn't waste any more time. "Here's my number," she said, handing her a pre-written slip of paper that had been waiting in her pocket. "If you decide to move forward, give me a call."

"Are you sure you want to stay here in this small town? Aren't you from..."

"Yes."

With that, Summer made her way out the door and to her second target. When she'd planned to visit Evan's coffee shop again today, she'd told herself it was just to get caffeinated. Something she should have done before going into the salon, apparently. It had nothing to do with sneaking another peek at him.

But now, with it clear that her aunt was being dragged through the mud, she really did only want one thing from him. Answers.

Was he the one leaving the scene of the crime? Did he have any dirt on Mrs. Peterson's new husband? Or her daughter and their possibly corrupt dealings with Mr. Hardy? Being the town barista, he had to hear things, right?

Was he as happily married as he seemed?

She kicked herself for that last one.

"Summer!" He called across the nearly full shop when she walked through the door. "What a perfect name, don't you think? You were meant to bring sunshine to our quiet little town."

Summer shook her head but couldn't help smiling. "Pretty sure California brings your sunshine. But funny you should say that. I was just talking to Mrs. Beesley about making my vacation a bit more permanent."

"Really? You bringing your butt kicking hair skills to Spring Harbor?" His face lit up and she tried hard not to notice the one dimple on his cheek.

"Maybe. Have to wait for her to get with Mr. Harding and Mrs. West about..."

"You just missed her."

"I what?"

"Jennifer. She just walked out. You had to pass her on the way in."

Summer had a few choice words for herself under her breath. She'd been so preoccupied thinking about seeing Evan again, she hadn't been paying attention.

Without another word, she took off running. She wasn't sure why, but she knew Marsha's daughter had the real answers to her questions. She just had to figure out how to get them out of her.

———

"What were you thinking?" Summer asked herself as she crouched behind a mail collection box in the middle of the sidewalk.

She was thinking that the best way to get information on who really killed Marsha Peterson was to follow the person closest to her. Her daughter.

What she wasn't thinking was how in the world she would do that without being seen. Which is how she found herself behind said mailbox, watching Jennifer West stroll toward a cute little inn across the street.

Like so many other buildings in this town, it looked like a cross between an adorable cottage and a mansion. Two things that shouldn't fit, but did so perfectly.

Summer stood and darted out toward the road as soon as the walking light turned green, and slammed into a tall, distinguished-looking gentleman. "Oh, so sorry! Are you OK?" she asked, even as she was the one tumbling backward.

He reached out a hand to grab her firmly by her elbow. Was everyone in this town strong as an ox? After steadying herself, Summer tried to pull her arm from him but he held tight. "Ms. Snow, I wasn't expecting to run into you like this. Rather awkward way to finally make your acquaintance."

From the villainous drawl and fake authoritative air, Summer knew immediately who she had run into. "Councilman Harding."

"One and the same." He reluctantly let go of her elbow and straightened his suit jacket. "You're making quite the name for yourself in our little town. What with the...incident... and now the call I recently received from Mrs. Beesley."

Summer's stomach clenched at his word choice. The *incident* was her name for what happened back home. For a split second, she thought that was what he was referring to. As if he'd somehow already known all her dirty little secrets. "Word travels fast. I just left her salon a few minutes ago." She tried and failed not to keep looking over his shoulder, toward the front door of the Inn. If she lost Jennifer now, she had no idea where to look next.

"Well, I do make it my business to know about my constituents and any interlopers that might be trying to weasel their way in." Only his eyes moved as he raked them over her, taking in her battered tennis shoes, decent enough shirt that still probably cost less than half of his pocket square, and her lack of hair or makeup. *Unworthy.* The thought was clearly written across his face.

"Weasel, you say?" She didn't care for him as much as he didn't care for her, so why should she bother remaining civil? The salon. That was why. She changed her tone and added, "I'm just enquiring at this stage, but yes, I'd like to discuss purchasing the salon at some point. I have a feeling Mrs. Beesley isn't as ready to leave as..."

"As her children are?"

Summer nodded.

"Well, let me handle that. My concern, however, is whether you have enough collateral to cover said offer. Given your recent troubles and transient lifestyle." Another long appraising look and practical sneer.

She wasn't about to remind him that the legal troubles were her aunt's, not hers. She felt guilty enough about the whole thing. And, honestly, she wasn't about to tell him exactly where she got the money for this down payment. Instead, she squared her shoulders and looked him in the eye. "My aunt is innocent and I will clear her name."

Councilman Harding didn't falter in his domination tactics. "Yes, well, that's good and all. However, the accusation alone could be enough to tarnish your reputation irreparably. Who in this town would trust you? Even if only with their hair?"

"The ones who saw what I did with my aunt's hair at the contest. And..." Summer racked her brain trying to remember the woman's name. "Mrs. Edwin, the mayor's wife. She and I just had a rather lovely chat, and let's just say, she's eternally grateful."

"Be that as it may...and we shall see if it is...I'm not sure our safe little town needs someone coming in from the big city to buy up all our property."

"You mean someone other than you?" Harding's eyes flared as the barb hit its mark. He wasn't the only one who knew how to google. "If you'll excuse me, I have somewhere better to be."

11

"The nerve of some people," Summer muttered under her breath as she crossed the street toward the Inn. After what she'd uncovered about Councilman Harding and how he made his real estate fortune, she had half a mind to go back there and give him another piece of her mind.

But she had more important things to do. So what if he had the ear of half the business owners in this town. And so what if he was the only person Mrs. Beesley would trust to advise her on the sale of the salon.

Maybe she was fooling herself by thinking it was a possibility, anyway. What made her think she could drop everything and move across the country to open her own hair salon? One week ago, she'd been a clerk at a prestigious law firm, climbing her way up a corporate ladder that had ruthlessly spit her out at its earliest convenience. This whole salon idea was a pipe dream, anyway.

She needed to focus. Her aunt's name was being dragged through the mud and it was up to her to clear it. She needed to speak to Jennifer, to find out what her mom had been working on, or just how much she trusted her hot new step-father. Anything that could lead her to the real killer and give her aunt back her freedom.

Summer paused outside the front door of the Inn, half admiring the antiquated charm, and half begging for Jennifer to still be inside.

"Welcome to the Manor House Inn," a bright, cheerful young woman said from behind the reception desk. "Are you checking in?"

"No, I..." Summer hesitated for just a moment as the plan formed. "I'm extending my stay but my current lodging will be unavailable. I was hoping you would have some sort of long-term rental I could book?"

"Why, yes. Happens all the time. Something about Spring Harbor makes it impossible to leave. I actually came here on a vacation three years ago and, well..." The woman smiled wide as she waved her hand to show how that story ended.

"It's so lovely. I'm fascinated by the architecture, too. How you manage to straddle the line between hip beach town and cozy village." Summer continued complimenting the inn and the town as she looked for Jennifer. She was not in the lobby, so either she had a room here or she was meeting someone who did. Someone who maybe wasn't her husband?

No, she shook that thought out of her head. She had no basis for such accusations. And what would it matter? Her having an affair wouldn't lead to her mother's death. Would it?

No sooner had the question left her mind, she caught a glimpse of Jennifer's arm rushing out a side door. Summer was sure it belonged to her, because she wore the same bangles as she'd noticed at the sheriff's office. Not only that, as the door closed on her, Summer was sure she saw a mass of dark hair, as if someone had been waiting there for her.

At first, she had the absurd thought that it was Mario, her new step-father. The hair looked quite dark, though that could have been the shadows. But was the thick waviness of it also a figment of her imagination?

No, that couldn't be it. Meeting her murdered mother's young husband at a hotel? However nice this place was, it didn't make sense.

Maybe it was Councilman Harding. Had her bumping into him been serendipitous? Or had he been following her? Coming to a clandestine meeting with Jennifer?

There was only one way to find out.

"Thank you! I have to go, but I'll call later to confirm." Summer took a card off the desk and shoved it in her pocket as she took off out the door.

She couldn't let them get away!

———

Summer raced to the back of the Inn, trying to see where Jennifer and her mystery man went, while also trying not to be seen by them or anyone else. She didn't know how suspicious she looked right now, but an outsider chasing locals around downtown had to be bad.

At the corner of the Inn, she stopped and leaned flat against the wall before peeking a head out. Jennifer was there, with her hand on the arm of a tall man. They were talking softly, too close to each other for her to make out the words. She was about to take a step closer when they both turned.

Jennifer and Drew Harding were coming right for her!

Summer twisted around until she was facing the opposite direction and began fiddling with her phone. She noticed a text from an unknown number and, though she would usually never respond to those, she clicked it.

> 'Hey, it's Alex. Your aunt and Carl came by my store and said you might be staying. That's wonderful! She gave me your number and literally said the words 'play date' so I think they want us to be friends'

Summer shook her head. She kind of remembered Alex from the cafe, and she liked her well enough, but for her aunt to go out searching for a friend for her...' *This is so embarrassing*'

There was a swish of fabric and stench of overbearing musky cologne as Jennifer and Drew passed by her. She didn't dare look up until they were well past her. Drew would have surely recognized her from their very recent confrontation. And Jennifer thought she was involved in her mom's death, so she would definitely recognize her.

'*I think it's sweet*' came Alex's reply.

Summer's thumbs hovered before typing. Drew hadn't been wearing cologne when they'd bumped into each other. So in the brief window between their encounter and his clandestine meeting with Jennifer, he'd slathered on half a bottle.

Interesting.

Finally, she replied, '*I suppose. Awkwardness aside, I'd love to hang out*'

With one eye on the phone and the other on the receding figures of Jennifer and Drew, Summer started walking. She hugged the wall as long as she could, though it didn't matter much now. They were in front of her and she should be in the clear.

Her phone buzzed. '*How about tonight? I close up at 7*'

> '*Perfect! I have a bunch of coupons to run through. Maybe you can help*'

> '*Yes! You have uncovered my ulterior motive. I'm just dying to get my hands on a BOGO chocolate waffle at Pancake Palace!*'

> '*Well now I am too! Meet you at 7:30?*'

She didn't wait for the confirmation before putting her phone back in her pocket. Jennifer and Drew ducked into a tavern a few doors down from Evan's coffee shop. Summer waited, counted to thirty, before going in. She hoped that would give them enough time to settle and not be paying attention to who was behind them.

The inside of the tavern was small but dark. Summer hoped the latter would make up for the former. She found Jennifer by the jangling of her bracelets. They were at a table against the side wall, Jennifer in the chair and Drew in the booth side. Any lingering doubts about his character faded. Of course he was the type to take the booth.

Summer slid into a table nearby and quickly ordered water with lemon to get rid of the waiter. After he'd gone, she realized how hungry she was from all that talk of chocolate waffles. But she couldn't risk ordering now. If they caught her or left, she had to be ready.

She leaned back, as if stretching, to get a better listen.

"I'm telling you, we can still get this done," Drew said. "This guy is in way over his head. He can't afford to keep the lights on much longer, not with my guys playing hardball. I bet if we hit him with fifteen under asking, he'll bite."

"But he isn't asking, remember? We came up with that number, which was already ten under his mortgage. I don't know. I think we need to lay..." Jennifer lowered her voice, so whatever she said next was unrecognizable.

Summer tried to lean farther, but the legs of her chair tipped and she slammed back down. Then she froze, waiting for one of them to come snatch her up. A long ten seconds passed before she dared lean back again, less conspicuously this time.

Drew was whispering back, but harshly enough that Summer could catch some of it. "...all we've been through... now or never...her legacy..."

"I'm well aware of what we've been through." Jennifer's answer was clipped and full of disgust. "And the only way it'll all be worth it is by taking this whole block at well...*well* below market value."

Summer couldn't believe her ears. They were going to push everyone on this block—including Evan—out of their businesses, and for way less money than they're worth.

Was the thing Jennifer and Drew have 'been through' the murder of her mother? Over what? Was she backing out of the deal? Did she know about them in the first place? So many thoughts swirled in Summer's head.

Maybe the ex-husband and the new one were both innocent. And Evan! She didn't think he was still on her list at all now. He was likely just another victim.

All of a sudden, this tavern was the last place Summer wanted to be. She was likely sitting right next to two murderers.

But before she could move, could get up and run screaming, Mario walked in the front door and went right to their booth.

12

Summer's pulse quickened. Her heartbeat pounded in her ears so hard she couldn't tell what they were saying. Was Mario in on this? Did he think they were cheating? Was he cheating with Jennifer? None of it made sense! And how did it all tie back to Marsha Peterson's death?

After a calming breath—or three, Summer leaned back in her chair again. Now, more than ever, she was desperate to hear what they had to say. But the more she strained, the more she only heard her own thrumming heartbeat.

So much for that breathing technique her mom had taught her.

"...not what you think," was all she could hear from Jennifer.

Summer risked leaning farther back and instantly regretted it.

Her phone fell and landed on the floor with a loud clang. Then it started vibrating even louder. She fumbled to pick it up, the phone buzzing and slipping through her fingers like something out of a bad TV show.

When she finally had it, Vanessa's voice rang through the whole tavern. "Girl! What are you doing? Can you hear me?"

Horrified, Summer looked at the puzzled face of her best friend on her screen. Somehow, in all her klutzy glory, she'd answered the call, switched it to video, *and* put it on speaker.

"Vanessa, hi," she whispered. "One sec."

Summer hung up the phone and texted.

'*Sorry, I'm at a restaurant. I dropped you*'

Yet again, she held her breath, expecting to be accosted at any moment.

'*Have you checked your socials yet?*'

'*You know I'm never on there. What's up?*'

'*People are blowing up my DMs trying to get to you. Answer them!*'

She didn't bother asking what they were blowing her up for. She also didn't bother checking. Social media was Vanessa's game. She wanted a quiet life.

The thought made her laugh.

Just a nice, quiet life in a small beach town, chasing murderers around.

Summer put her phone in her pocket and dared a glance over her shoulder.

The booth was empty. They'd given her the slip!

She dropped a five-dollar bill on the table and got up, ready to give chase again.

"I wouldn't do that if I were you."

———

Evan loomed over her with a stern look on his face.

"What are you...Shouldn't do what?" She caught herself and recovered.

"I saw you following them."

Summer stumbled back. "Were you following *me*?"

He nearly laughed. "You're kinda hard to miss."

She wasn't sure what he meant by that, or whether she liked his tone.

"Seriously, they're bad news. All of them. You need to be more careful."

Evan pulled out the seat across from her and sat down. Given no choice, Summer did the same, plopping back in the chair she'd just vacated. "I'm not the only one who should be careful," she said. "They're gunning for your coffee shop. The whole block!"

"I know."

"You're rather calm for someone who's about to lose his business..."

Or was he?

Had she been too hasty to remove him from her suspect list? And why? Because he was handsome? And flirty? What a detective she would make!

"I've known for a long time," he continued, picking at her straw wrapper. "They've come after me many times since..." He trailed off, not finishing that thought. Instead, he dropped the straw and placed his hands on the table. "I have never wavered, and I don't plan on starting now. I will not sell."

That just confused her more.

Was he chivalrous? Standing up to the snakes trying to take over their town? Or was he telling her to be careful, not because of Drew and his cronies, but because of himself? What was he willing to do to save his coffee shop?

"I didn't plan on buying the coffee shop, not at first." The look in his eyes as he said the last part made her heart skip and start pounding again. Evan held her gaze as he said, "I came here two summers ago to care for my mother..."

Summer gasped.

She didn't have to ask. She could tell by the way his voice caught in his throat how that had ended.

"She knew the previous owner and...seeing her go through her illness, he'd decided to retire early. I took over, on a temporary basis, just to earn a little cash to help my mom out, until he could find a permanent buyer. But..."

A wavering smile spread across his face. "I fell in love."

The words hit her harder than she expected, and she didn't like the sour feeling they gave her in the pit of her stomach.

Evan shrugged. "I bought the place and I've been here ever since."

It all made sense. He'd been in the same position she found herself in now. Floundering, lost...ready to make a change in his life.

"And you can't bear to think of selling to...them," Summer said, nodding.

"Never. Especially now. My sister, Rose and my niece, Daisy...you met them at the campground. They came to pick up my mom's ashes and...they fell in love, too. I couldn't sell now. Not after seeing the joy on Daisy's face when she saw the name of the place."

Summer's mouth went dry. "The name?"

Now Evan beamed. "Spring in Your Step? That's what my mom said every morning when I made her a cup of coffee. 'That'll put a spring in your step, Evan!'"

Summer smiled as warmth filled her chest.

His sister and niece.

13

The next day, Summer hit the road bright and early again. She'd had a hard time sleeping, what with everything that she'd seen and heard with Jennifer, Mario, and Drew Harding. Not to mention her riveting conversation with Evan that had lasted well into the evening.

Time had gotten so away from her, she didn't even notice she was starving until Alex texted about their waffle plans. The buzz of her phone had broken whatever spell she and Evan had been under, and he'd quickly begged her forgiveness for taking up so much of her time. After warning her, yet again, to stay clear of *those three*, he disappeared.

And, whether from exhaustion or sadness upon seeing him go, she hadn't felt much like waffles. So she'd promised a rain check for tonight and gone back to the RV for peanut butter and jelly...and a stern talk with her aunt about play dates.

But now, as she parked Aunt Clara's bright yellow punch buggy outside the Spring Harbor Municipal Complex—really just two buildings smooshed together and repainted to look like they belonged that way—she couldn't let herself think about anything other than the matter at hand. As she was getting out of the car, about to feed the meter, a shadow moved behind her.

"Miss Snow."

Summer spun around to find Evan standing over her, much as she'd found him the day before. His hair was still wet, slicked back with one wayward curl hanging over his eye. With his model looks and that rakish grin, she almost forgot that he'd been following her.

Almost.

"Do you make a habit of sneaking up behind women?"

"Only when they need it."

Summer huffed. "I think you have me confused with..."

"With the *other* woman who I found following the most dangerous man in town yesterday?"

"I'm just here to discuss the salon deal. He's the only one Mrs. Beesley will listen to." It wasn't totally a lie, though Summer didn't care much about explaining herself to him, or anyone for that matter. She yanked her card out of the meter and began to walk off, then turned back. "How did you know I was here?"

"I'd rather not say."

"Either you say or we stand here on the side of the road looking like idiots."

Evan shrugged. "That works for me."

Summer groaned and started walking, then picked up her pace. She didn't think she could outrun Evan, not with his long legs, but she aimed to make him work for it. "Did my aunt put you up to this?"

Even after the argument last night, she wouldn't have put it past Aunt Clara to still butt in and ask Evan to protect her today.

"No."

She glared at him.

"Not *her* per se."

"Well you tell Carl, per se, that I don't need a big strong man to keep me safe on the mean streets of Spring Harbor!"

"Big and strong?" The satisfaction in his voice made Summer's cheeks burn.

Summer swung open the door to the municipal building and did not hold it for Evan. "Drew Harding, please?"

"Councilman Harding has a very full schedule today. I'm afraid he..."

Evan flashed a badge, causing both the receptionist and Summer's mouths to hang open.

"Yes, of course, officer. I will let him know you are here."

When the woman hurried away, Summer spun on Evan as he was folding his wallet and putting it back in his pocket. "You're a *cop*?"

"I never said that."

"Then what-"

"My neighborhood watch back in Delaware took its job very seriously."

"You are...so..."

"Big and strong?"

Summer didn't get the chance to dash his hopes before Drew Harding interrupted them. "Ms. Snow, Mr. Larson...I must admit, I hadn't expected to see the two of you together."

Stifling the urge to say 'me neither,' Summer followed Drew Harding into his office. It was as lavish and gaudy as she had imagined.

"Shall we cut to the chase?" He lingered on the last word as if letting her know she'd been made the day before. He knew she was following them.

Still, she kept up her ruse. "Gladly. I'm sure by now you've worked up the numbers on the salon. I'm here to-"

"The salon, right? I'm afraid I did not have time to work up any numbers. What with my business partner's untimely death and all. It seems I've had my hands full, dissolving corporations and all to comply with the rules of her estate."

Summer knew this was a half truth but did not let on. She'd already learned that Mr. Harding worked with both Marsha and Jennifer on his shady deals. Mario...she'd yet to decide where he played into all this. Somewhere between a coldblooded murderer and grieving husband.

"Of course. I would expect nothing less from a man of your...reputation. However, I have decided that I will be staying in Spring Harbor for the foreseeable future and..."

"*You* have decided?"

"Yes. I have decided that this particular outsider is exactly what this town needs. Someone who won't be so easily pushed around or dismissed by...people who may or may not have their own reasons for dissolving corporations after the *untimely* death of their partner."

––––––

As soon as they reached the courtyard outside Harding's office, Evan clapped his hand to his chest. "What was all that? I thought he was going to fly out of that chair and strangle you."

They both blanched at his choice of words.

"I told you I didn't need a knight in shining armor." Summer opened her car door and climbed in before realizing that Evan had done the same. She looked across at him, now sitting in the passenger seat of her aunt's little punch buggy. "What are you doing?"

"I walked here," was his only explanation.

Summer glanced at the nonexistent space between the top of his head and the roof of the car. "You look ridiculous."

"You look..." He slammed his mouth shut and Summer didn't like just how much she needed to know what he'd been about to say.

She peeled out of the parking spot before she could ask.

After five minutes of silence, which was somehow both awkward and comfortable, Evan asked, "Seriously, what do you have on him?"

"Do you not know what he's been up to? He's your councilman?"

"I was...focused on other things."

Every bit of feigned animosity she'd been carrying dissipated. "I'm sorry." When he didn't say anything, she told him what she knew. "Mr. Harding was run out of his last town for doing exactly what he's doing here. He 'resigned' from his post as treasurer halfway through his term and skipped town, owing a lot of money to a lot of worse people than him."

"So if his partner ended up dead, and he was forced to liquidate his companies, he'd stand to gain a small fortune. More than enough to pay back his debts."

Summer laughed. "If he was the type to pay them back, yes. Though I'm sure he'd much rather turn that small fortune into a bigger one off the backs of the honest, working-class people of Spring Harbor."

"Well, knight in shining armor or not, I'm glad I went with you. If he's really that dirty...and now he knows you know... he could have..."

Summer gasped.

"What?"

She pulled the punch buggy over and jumped out of the car.

"What are you doing? You're gonna get run over!"

Summer didn't stop. All she cared about was the tiny little puppy shivering on the side of the road. She scooped him up and hugged him to her. It was still autumn and the day promised to be warm enough, but the poor little thing trembled in her arms like it was the dead of winter.

She went to the passenger side of the car and motioned for Evan to open the door. As soon as he had, she nodded for him to get out. "You're driving."

Evan didn't argue, and once he was behind the wheel, he asked, "Is he alright?"

"I think so. Just scared. Poor fella." Summer cooed at the puppy, which she could now tell was a beagle. She ran her finger over the white line of fur between his brows, then down the adorably long brown ear nestled to her chest. "I think I'm in love."

"Can you feel a chip? At the scruff of his neck?"

"No."

Evan pulled into his reserved spot in front of the coffee shop. "Come on. Get him inside."

"You sure?"

"I know the owner. He's a really nice guy. He won't mind."

Summer rolled her eyes, but was glad to let him lead her and the puppy to the counter. He set out a plate of ham and bacon, along with a bowl of water. They both watched the puppy devour every bite.

It took way too long for Summer to realize they were the only ones in the shop. "Where is everyone?"

Evan shrugged.

"You closed your store to follow me?"

"No. Didn't open it."

"Same difference."

He shrugged again, this time with a smile. "Well then, would you do me the honor of being my first customer?"

"Yes, please. I would kill for a cup of coffee right now."

"Or you could let me show you how to make it instead."

Summer looked down at the puppy, now curled up under her stool. His fat belly rose and fell with every snore.

"He'll be fine. Here, let me show you how to make a Cozy Campfire." He took her hand and tugged her behind the counter. "The key is getting the ratio of toasted marshmallow and cinnamon sprinkles just right."

After the coffee was poured, Evan let her hold the foaming wand and attempt to create a design. It did not go well.

"I think I'll stick to cutting hair."

Evan appraised the foam blob. "Yeah, I believe that would be best. Though, I suppose now you owe me a cut...in exchange for the barista lesson."

With a laugh that didn't sound as chipper as she'd meant, Summer said, "Absolutely. If I ever get the shop, or even a job. If not, I'll be back on the road once Aunt Clara leaves for her ski trip. Though I have no idea where I'll go from here."

"Well, we can't let that happen, can we?" His expression, too, wasn't as light as she expected he meant for it to be.

"We?"

He nodded toward the still sleeping puppy. "Me and..."

"Barney."

Neither of them could stifle their giggles.

"Right. Me and Barney will make it so you couldn't bear to leave us."

"I already can't bear it. To leave...him..." She stumbled on every word like a fool.

"And I couldn't bear to see...him...go." Evan threw up his hands. "So, I'll talk with Mrs. Beesley. Put in a good word. We'll get you that salon."

"And how do you plan on doing that?"

He flashed her his best movie star smile.

"I don't think your manly charms will work on Mrs. Beesley."

"My manly charm always works."

"Always?"

He gave her another shrug. "It's true." Then he lowered his voice. "It's also true that I don't want you to leave."

Summer didn't know what to say to that, so she said the only thing she'd been thinking for days. "I have to clear my aunt's name first, or I won't be allowed to leave."

"Mine, too."

She raised her eyebrows in confusion. Was he on the sheriff's suspect list, too?

Evan grinned wider than his movie star smile. "Sheriff Brady paid me a visit yesterday. It seems I'm on his radar now, after someone mentioned a 'devilishly handsome man' leaving the scene of the crime."

14

Summer waited in the parked car, giving Barney a pep talk about using the new potty pads she'd just bought. It was only then that she realized she'd never warned Aunt Clara about their new roommate. In fact, they hadn't spoken all day. Strange, but probably expected, after the stunt she and Carl pulled that morning.

"Alright, let's do this. Remember, be cute! Use those puppy dog eyes to our advantage." She got out of the car and grabbed Barney, then all the stuff in the back seat—which may have been slightly more than just potty pads.

It took longer than expected, and Summer noticed that the porch light wasn't on. Another sign of her aunt's mood? She wasn't sure.

Then, when she finally made it to the door, her irritated amusement turned to cold, hard fear. Not only was the porch light off, it was shattered. Glass littered the ground around the steps. And the door was wide open.

"Aunt Clara!"

Summer dropped everything but Barney and ran inside. The whole place was trashed. Cabinets were open and the items strewn about the floor. Nearly all of Aunt Clara's knick knacks were toppled and broken. Even the bathroom door had been yanked off its hinges and was leaning across the hallway.

"Aunt Clara! Aunt Clara!" Summer called and called, but there was no answer. She put Barney inside her shirt and tucked the bottom into her pants. "This is gonna get bumpy," she told him before stepping on the bathroom door. When she finally crawled over it, she flung open the thin partition to her aunt's bedroom. It, too, was trashed...but empty.

"Aunt Clara!"

She looked under the bed, the pile of clothes and things tossed in the corner, behind another partition her aunt used for changing clothes.

When she was out of places to look, Summer ran back out the door and straight for Carl's. She banged on the whole side of the RV to get his attention on her way to his door. It swung open before she got there.

"She's in here!" Carl waved Summer in and Aunt Clara was standing right behind him.

Summer gave her aunt a hug so tight, Barney yelped.

Everyone looked down at her wriggling midsection, including Sheriff Brady.

Aunt Clara poked the lump trying to get out of Summer's shirt. "Whatcha got there?"

"Are you alright? I was so worried! Your RV is..."

"I'm fine, sweetie. Luckily, I was out with Carl when it happened. We came back to find it like that and Carl called the Sheriff. I hope you didn't touch anything."

Summer looked down at her hands and memories of crawling over the door and tossing things aside to look for her aunt flashed through her mind. "I...I think I touched everything."

Aunt Clara smiled and pulled her close again. "It's alright. Sheriff Brady here already had a look."

Sheriff Brady nodded. "Where were you all day?"

"Out," she said, not wanting to give Aunt Clara and Carl the satisfaction of knowing she'd spent the whole day with Evan.

"Well, I'm gonna need a more detailed report than that. How about you come back to the..."

"No!" Summer's answer was louder than she'd meant, and Barney cried out.

Aunt Clara put a hand on her hip. "Girl, what is that thing?"

Summer smiled and pulled the puppy out of her shirt. "Aunt Clara, meet Barney."

Sheriff Brady scribbled on his notepad.

Summer nodded toward him. "Yes, I was out rescuing this cute little guy off the side of the road." She looked at her aunt and barely stifled the urge to ask, 'Can I keep him?' like a child.

"Oh, he's precious." Aunt Clara practically snatched Barney from Summer. Maybe convincing her to let him stay might not be as hard as she thought.

"Do you know who did it?" Summer asked Sheriff Brady.

"Too soon to tell."

"And I can't tell if anything's missing. Not with that mess."

"Well, whatever isn't missing is sure broken. They destroyed everything!"

"It can be replaced," Aunt Clara said, patting Summer on the arm while she and Carl let Barney lick them all over.

Summer turned to face Sheriff Brady and put her hands on her hips. "Is this proof enough that my aunt had nothing to do with Mrs. Peterson's murder? She's innocent! And someone's trying to intimidate us."

Sheriff Brady closed his notebook and stuffed it in his pocket before saying, "Or it could have been someone trying to find evidence to help convict her."

"You have got to be kidding me!" Summer blew up and got in the sheriff's face, but Carl pulled her back.

"I've already had a similar discussion with the sheriff. He promised that all avenues of investigation shall be fully explored. And...until you're allowed to leave, I promised I would keep a closer eye on both of you." The smile on Carl's face when he said that last part made Summer nervous.

"And?"

"And since you *can't* leave town, I have a date to the Fall Ball tomorrow. We just need to get you-"

"Do *not* finish that sentence."

———

"How about this?" Summer held up the top half of a horse figurine.

Aunt Clara, who had taken up a spot on the small couch to play with Barney and 'supervise' the clean up of her RV, waved a hand. "That one was a present from Charlie? You remember him? I never really…"

"Toss it!" Carl called from the hallway, where he was replacing the bathroom door.

"Oh, Carl. You're much cuter than he ever was. Don't be jealous!" Aunt Clara smiled and waved again, then whispered, "Toss it."

Summer's brows shot up. She had never heard her aunt be so…affectionate with any of her male friends in the past.

"Didn't doubt it for a second," was Carl's hearty reply.

"You two are insufferable. I need some fresh air."

"Wait," Aunt Clara said, "make sure my papers are in order first." She pointed to a stack of paper at the back of the kitchen table.

Summer picked up the first few pages and started reading, when something gold caught her eye. On the table beside the stack was a business card with shiny gold lettering. She knew before she touched it what it was. She recognized the logo.

"Why do you have a business card from Drew Harding's real estate company?"

"I don't."

Summer picked it up and showed it to her aunt.

"That wasn't there before. There's no way I'd ever talk to that man and certainly never invite him into my home."

Carl snatched the card from Summer. The anger he'd been barely keeping under the surface bubbled over and his face turned red. "I'll kill him!"

"Guys, I think this is all my fault." Summer sank onto the kitchen booth. "I didn't just go to his office this morning to talk about the salon."

"What?" Aunt Clara asked. "You went to see him?"

Summer and Carl exchanged looks. He hadn't told her aunt what she'd been up to.

"Don't worry. I had a bodyguard." Summer's next glance at Carl lasted several long seconds. "But I also...might have... followed him a little yesterday."

"Oh, Summer. Sweetie." Aunt Clara put out her arms and Summer went to her. "Please don't put yourself in danger like that on my account."

Summer took the spot on the small couch beside her aunt and let the older woman hold her, while Barney snuggled between them.

"I was trying to clear your name. And I wasn't actually following him, not at first anyway. I saw Marsha's daughter, Jennifer, and started following her. And I bumped into Harding...literally."

Aunt Clara took a deep breath and patted Summer's back.

Carl came over to stand in front of them, then paced back and forth. "You must have spooked him."

"He deserves it. I saw him and Jennifer meet *at a hotel*! Then I followed them to a little tavern and heard some of what they were discussing. They want to buy up the whole downtown block for next to nothing. They'll push everyone out. Evan. Mrs. Beesley. Alex!"

Upon hearing herself say Alex's name, she remembered they were supposed to meet for waffles. She hated to postpone again, but she couldn't leave Aunt Clara like this. Not now. She took out her phone and texted Alex, begging for another raincheck, while Carl and Aunt Clara discussed their next steps.

"Oh," Summer said after receiving Alex's reply text; a sad face and thumb's up. "Mario was there, too. What would he be doing with them? He wasn't part of the business, was he?"

Carl shrugged. "I don't think so. They hadn't been married that long. But...I'll check with my contacts at the station. They probably can't tell me much, but I'll get what info I can. Anything to help."

"In the meantime..." Aunt Clara handed Barney to Summer and stood up. "We should let the cops do their thing and enjoy our couple of days together." She rifled through the papers and held up a bright orange and brown flyer with the words "Fall Ball" typed across it in a giant font.

Summer shook her head. "I already told you. I'm not going."

Aunt Clara acted as if she didn't even hear her. She just kept pointing to all the fun stuff. "Carl, you know I have to try bobbing for apples. I used to be so good at it. I bet I can still..."

"Aunt Clara!" Summer stood up. "The last thing I want to do is go to another event at this place."

Aunt Clara looked past Carl and straight into Summer's eyes. "It's not *this place's* fault. And we are going. I already told Carl to have Evan ask you-"

"You did what?"

15

The next day, as if she hadn't learned her lesson the hard way, Summer was up before Aunt Clara and out the door...after a quick cuddle with Barney and a note that she'd be back shortly. She thought about lying that she needed to get more puppy things from the store, but considering how much she'd bought the day before, she knew that wouldn't fly.

She'd barely made it to her stakeout spot when her phone rang.

"I'll be back soon, I promise," she whispered to Aunt Clara.

"I thought we said we were done with this craziness."

"You said. I was noticeably quiet. Nothing's gonna happen. I'm in public." Summer hung up before Aunt Clara could argue that Marsha Peterson had been in public when she was killed.

She looked around the lobby of The Manor House Inn, keeping one eye on the door that Jennifer had snuck out of, and the other on the place itself. Could this really be her new temporary home? If she cleared her aunt's name and decided to stay in town, would she like living here?

The brochure she had swiped at the front door to cover her face sure made it seem that way. Despite the quaint, old-world exterior, it had all the amenities she would ever ask for. A gym—not that she'd use it, a pool—she would definitely use, and a lounge in the courtyard. When thoughts of a quiet dinner with Evan crept into her mind, she quickly folded the brochure.

Just in time to see a figure coming down the hallway.

She held the brochure back up and peeked over it, and watched Mario put on a pair of sunglasses and walk out the door.

Summer couldn't hide her shock, but clamped a hand over her mouth to keep the gasp from alerting him to her presence.

Why would he be at the Inn? At *any* hotel? He had a home right here in town. And of all the places he could choose to stay besides his own home, he picked the same inn where she'd followed Jennifer to yesterday?

Only one way to find out!

Summer dropped the brochure and followed Mario out.

She immediately recognized the path he was taking. It was the same way Jennifer and Drew had gone the other day. Only this time, instead of turning into the tavern, he went right for Evan's coffee shop.

Summer didn't have long to come up with a plan. So she ducked inside and hoped Evan was too busy to notice her. It was, in fact, busy in the shop, but he saw her anyway. He smiled and began to say something until he must have caught the look on her face...or the way she knew she was crouching like a cat burglar in broad daylight. Then his expression turned to one of concern.

"Hey!" A bright, cheery voice startled Summer and her eyes went straight to Mario.

He'd seen her. He ripped off his sunglasses to be sure, then jumped up from his seat.

"I'm so glad I ran into you!" Alex was still talking, and moved between Summer and the door. "Maybe we can skip waffles and..."

Summer leapt up and tried to give chase, but couldn't get around Alex.

Then she heard a scuffle at the door and looked up. Evan was blocking Mario from exiting. His body language wasn't confrontational, and he had his hands out to calm Mario, but his foot was in the way, nonetheless.

"Hey, man, we just want to talk."

"Who are you?" Mario kept looking between Evan and Summer. "What's going on?"

Alex's face was pure shock and she easily let Summer move her out of the way. Summer went to the door and put her hands out to Mario in the same way Evan had. "We just want to talk. About..." She froze. She hadn't expected to get this far. And didn't know how to bring up the subject of his wife's death.

Evan had no such reservations. "My friend and her aunt are caught up in the investigation into your wife's death and we'd like some answers."

Mario whipped around to face Summer. "You?"

"I didn't do it! And neither did my aunt. I'm just trying to clear her name."

"Well I didn't do it either! And I'm just trying to get out of this crazy town!"

Evan gestured slowly for everyone to just calm down. "Look, everyone knows the husband is the prime suspect in something like this. But you're lucky..." Mario's glare made him backtrack. "I mean, you weren't the only husband who happened to be in town that night. So if you didn't do it, what do you know about her ex?"

Mario shook his head. "Frank was here visiting Jennifer. She asked him to come because she was having some personal troubles. He's...he's a good guy. I didn't kill my wife and neither did he. I'm not throwing him under the bus to save myself. I just want it all to go away."

Mario pushed past Evan, who stepped aside and let him go.

"Is this why you've been blowing me off?" Alex said, her eyes still bulging from shock.

———

That evening, despite her best efforts, Summer found herself in a dress at the pavilion, watching pumpkin lights twinkle overhead. She'd promised Aunt Clara to stop investigating for one night and to have fun, though she thought asking for both those things was asking for too much.

She waved at Alex across the dance floor and smiled. After explaining everything, Alex had forgiven her and they'd permanently rainchecked their waffle dinner until after Aunt Clara's name was cleared.

Thinking of it made Summer laugh. She sure was making a lot of future promises for a girl who was about to be homeless. She had no plans after this. Nowhere to go. No way to earn a living.

As if on cue, Mrs. Beesley's round face popped up right in front of her. "Ms. Snow."

"Hi, Mrs. Beesley," Summer said with a polite nod. She'd given up on her pipe dream of owning the shop. And she actually felt bad for Mrs. Beesley. If Drew Harding had his way, she would only be selling that shop to him, at a fraction of its worth.

"Did you speak to Mr. Harding about the property?" Mrs. Beesley asked.

Summer only nodded.

"Didn't like his numbers?" The older woman's eyebrow rose nearly high enough to disappear under her beehive.

"Never even got that far," Summer said, and she was about to excuse herself when Mrs. Beesley caught her arm.

"I expected as much. But I have a proposition for you. If this whole murder mess dies down, I'd be open to giving you a job at the salon. Mrs. Edwin was quite impressed with you the other day. And anyone who can get her to change her mind about anything...well, you'd be an asset."

"She'll take it!" Aunt Clara said, appearing at Summer's side before she could respond.

Mrs. Beesley looked down at Aunt Clara, then at the poorly hidden puppy in her dress jacket. "Yes, well, lovely. I'll have a spot open for you next week."

"Thank you," Summer said.

Then, Mrs. Beesley looked as if she was about to go, but stopped herself. "If things had worked out and you'd worked out a deal with Mr. Harding, what would you have done with the space?"

Summer closed her eyes for a moment, then described her dream salon. "I'd have pixie lights strung along pale green and yellow walls with hand-painted flowers. Soft, retro chairs and plants everywhere."

When Summer opened her eyes, the look on Mrs. Beesley's face was one of horror. The woman walked off without another word.

Summer bent down to kiss Barney, still wriggling in her aunt's jacket pocket, and let the puppy's excitement for the evening wash away some of her dejection. "I think I'm gonna get more punch."

Aunt Clara nodded, a smile forming on her lips.

When Summer turned around, she bumped right into Evan. Part of her had been hoping she wouldn't see him tonight, after their terribly awkward discussion of her aunt and Carl's matchmaking attempt. But a bigger part of her had been wishing for this exact moment.

Although, in her imagination, he didn't have a woman and child in tow.

"Summer! I'd like you to meet Rose, my sister, and my niece, Daisy. Guys, this is Summer."

She shook his sister's hand and smiled down at his niece. "Nice to meet you."

"Evan's told us so much-"

"How did you make that lady's hair stand up so good?" Daisy interrupted.

Summer bent down and whispered, "My own special mixture of hair spray and mousse. It's hard to get out though. If I show you how to do it, you can only use it with your mom's permission."

After yet another promise to give more hairstyling tips, the adults settled into a quiet, careful discussion about the case.

"I don't know," Summer said after a few minutes of back and forth. "I can't shake the fact that Mario was at the Inn when he has his own place. And the same inn where Jennifer was staying. It's too coincidental. And if the stereotype is true, that it's always the husband, do you think they were..." She leaned in and whispered, "...having an affair?"

Rose shook her head. "If my husband died in our house I would never step foot in it again."

"I hadn't thought of that," Summer said. And she hadn't.

If Mario had a perfectly good explanation for being at the Inn, what else had she been looking at the wrong way?

16

Summer was considering Evan's sister's words when something across the pavilion caught her eye. "Look at that," she whispered to Evan, trying not to point too noticeably.

Though, as soon as she said it, he turned fully around and asked, "What?" so loudly that Summer was sure the whole RV park heard him.

"What are they doing here?" Summer guided Evan by the arm until he was facing the group in the corner. Sheriff Brady, Drew Harding, Mario, and Jennifer were all huddled together, discussing something that looked important.

"Weird," Evan said.

"Very. Why would someone with their money be hanging around an RV park, especially if what your sister said is true? If Mario can't bear to be in the house he shared with Marsha, he certainly wouldn't want to come back to the scene of the crime."

Something about that line struck a chord. Wasn't that what always got a murderer caught? Returning to the scene of the crime? Did that mean one of them really was the killer?

No, by that logic, she and Aunt Clara were also still on the guilty radar, because here they were, too.

"Cover me," she said, letting go of Evan's arm and moving to the edge of the pavilion.

"No," Evan hissed. "Get back here."

Summer kept going as if she couldn't hear him.

"How am I supposed to ask you to dance with me if you're dead?"

That worked. She stopped and turned back. "You're not," she whispered. "And I won't be dead. We're in public," she said, repeating the words her aunt had tried to use on her. Hopefully it worked this time.

Summer mingled with a few people on her way to the corner of the pavilion. She tried answering their polite questions about her aunt's winning hairstyle in the contest and field other, less veiled, attempts at finding out information on the investigation. She fought the urge to tell them she was trying to find those answers herself, if she could just get closer.

By the time she did make it over to the group, it had grown by two. The Beesley twins stood beside Drew Harding. Summer noticed that Ramona's blue pants suit was nearly identical to Mrs. Beesley's. Maybe they were twins after all.

"...get you a much better deal with financing in house..." Harding was saying.

By the look on Mrs. Beesley's face, Summer didn't think she was as receptive to the offer as Harding probably hoped.

Sheriff Brady excused himself, giving Summer a better look at Jennifer...and at Mario. She tried to discern the body language between them. Were they standing too close? Glancing at each other a bit too long?

She honestly couldn't tell. And she didn't like where that left her and Aunt Clara. No closer to the truth.

She was, however, too close to a giant blow-up cornucopia decoration, which she stumbled into and let out a loud gasp. She just knew she'd been busted, and dared to look up, but before she could...

A large hand clamped down on her shoulder.

––––––

"You scared me!" Summer gasped. She spun around to find Evan standing over her.

"Good! I told you not to."

Summer hurried away before Harding or any of his buddies heard them. But Evan did not let go. Instead, he pulled her toward the makeshift dance floor.

"You told me?" Summer answered, incredulous, as they moved with the music. She was at war with herself, here in his arms. He had helped her tremendously and saved her butt more than once already. But...she had to admit she still hadn't removed him from her suspect list. Not completely. Though he hadn't done anything suspicious. Irritating, yes. But not suspicious.

"Have a bit more gratitude. I'm saving you from yourself right now. Your clumsy, adorable self." He smiled down at her, then twirled her out and back in with the ease of a professional dancer.

Despite her growing ire, she couldn't help but ask, "Where did you learn how to dance?"

"Good, huh? Too bad there isn't a contest for this. With *two* coupon books, we'd be unstoppable!" Evan pulled her to him, his hand on her back strong and confident.

"That wasn't an answer."

"Look," Evan said with a nod toward the corner. "What do you think of those two?" He spun them around so she could get a better look.

Jennifer was leaning against the pavilion's wooden column and watching Mario intently as he spoke to the sheriff. Mario had his hands clasped in front of him and his weight on his opposite leg.

"Do you see what I see?" Evan asked. When she shrugged, he continued. "I'm not sure about her, but he clearly has no interest."

"How can you tell?"

Evan leaned in close. "It's obvious. He isn't even looking at her, for one. I haven't seen them touch once. He's turned away from her. He's closed off. Totally not interested."

Summer let his words sink in as he led her around the pavilion and the music swelled between them. The more she thought about the things Jennifer and Mario weren't doing, the more she realized they were exactly the things she and Evan were.

She let go of Evan's hand and pushed back. "I..."

She darted off before finishing the sentence.

17

S ummer hurried to where her aunt and Carl were standing, grabbed Barney, and busied herself with cuddling him.

"Where's Evan?" Aunt Clara asked too sweetly.

"How should I know?"

Carl snickered. "Gather any good intelligence?"

"You were watching us—me?"

Aunt Clara took Barney back. "Only because I knew you couldn't keep your word and let the investigation go for one night. You're your mother's daughter, that's for sure."

Summer lifted her chin in the air. "I'll be sure to tell her you said that. And I wouldn't have been so curious if they weren't whispering in the corner like a bunch of conspirators."

"Yes," Carl agreed. "They do seem suspicious, don't they?"

"Couldn't agree more," Evan's deep voice said from behind her. He sounded out of breath as if he'd chased her across the pavilion.

Summer didn't dare look at him. She wished she hadn't allowed Aunt Clara to take back the puppy. She needed something to do with her hands.

As the song they'd been dancing to wound down, the lights around the pavilion flashed.

"Ope," Carl said, taking Aunt Clara's arm. "Last dance!"

They disappeared in the crowd of partygoers, leaving Summer and Evan standing too close.

"Do you want to-"

She didn't let him finish the thought. "Watch my aunt," she said, and disappeared in the other direction.

Summer couldn't shake the bad feeling in the pit of her stomach. And when she found the corner where Harding had been holding court empty, that bad feeling was confirmed. She scanned the pavilion, then the ones behind it. When she caught sight of the Rec Room, she shook out the memory of seeing Marsha's body on its floor.

But as she refocused, she saw three sets of lights turn on in the parking lot. One, she was sure, belonged to Sheriff Brady's patrol car. The other two, she needed to get a closer look.

As had become a habit with her lately, Summer pressed herself into the shadows and snuck closer. Jennifer and Drew stood together beside a dark sedan. From the way they leaned in toward each other, she could tell they were whispering, though nobody seemed to be near. Whatever they were discussing must have been intense, because both had their fingers in the other's face.

Summer inched closer, revealing more of herself than she wanted to, but she felt certain they were too engrossed in their conversation to notice.

Until a sound off to Summer's left made all three of them jump.

Another figure emerged from the shadows, and it looked an awful lot like Mario. He glared at the two standing by their cars, looking livid.

Spooked, Jennifer and Drew both got into the same car and drove away. Off to Summer's left, Mario's car also cranked up and pulled out.

Summer froze. She couldn't lose any of them, but now risked losing all.

————

Summer had to think quickly.

As she ran to her aunt's RV to get the car, she thought back to the look on Mario's face as he watched Jennifer and Drew whispering. That, and the conversation she had with Evan, led her to believe he was not involved. He was just as suspicious of those two as she was. Summer marked Mario off her mental list of suspects and focused on her target.

She worried their dark sedan would be too hard to follow, especially with their head start. Her only saving grace would be how many people were at this dance. Maybe there would be so few cars on the road, theirs would stick out.

As she pulled out of the RV park, there was one set of lights on the road, and Summer turned to follow them. If she was wrong about this, she might lose her only chance to find out what was really going on in this town.

It didn't take long for her to catch up to the car and realize where they were headed. A fact that only solidified her gut feeling that she was on the right track.

The black sedan turned right onto Main and pulled into a back alley behind Mrs. Beesley's salon.

Summer waited as long as she could before getting out and following them. She crouched behind a dumpster, holding her breath and wishing their clandestine meeting would take place somewhere less disgusting.

But her sneaking paid off, because their voices bounced around the empty alley and she was close enough to hear all of it.

"I will not pay that much for this place," Jennifer was snapping in Drew Harding's direction.

"You won't have to. Trust me." Drew clicked the button on his key fob and popped the trunk.

"Because trusting you has done me so many favors lately." Jennifer pulled her jacket tight across her chest.

"Do you want that outsider coming in here and messing up our entire plan? Or do you want to help me?"

"Why don't we just take care of *her*?"

"In due time. Right now, we have to let my associates finish what they started and I promise you, this place won't be worth half what I offered."

Suddenly, a hand clamped down hard on Summer's shoulder. She didn't know how Evan had found her, but she was glad. Something told her she would need his help yet again.

She turned with a smile.

18

Summer's smile faded as it took her too long to figure out who belonged to the hand on her shoulder.

"Sheriff Brady! You scared me. But you're just in time."

"Always. And what might I ask are you doing back here?"

Summer turned back toward the alleyway, hoping to catch Jennifer and Drew in whatever dirty deeds they were up to. She still hadn't figured it out yet, but she knew it was bad.

But they were gone.

Sheriff Brady didn't let go of Summer's shoulder. Instead, he led her by it over to where Drew and Jennifer had been standing. In their place, partially hidden in the building's shadow, was a gas can.

"That's not good," Summer whispered.

"No, I suppose it's not. Seeing as how I got a call for a prowler and when I come to check it out, here you are. And there that is." He pointed to the gas can as if Summer needed it to be spelled out for her.

"I didn't...I wasn't...That's not mine."

"Rather a strange coincidence, don't you think?" Sheriff Brady let Summer's shoulder go, finally, and walked over to the gas can. He crouched down and shined his light on it. Summer noticed, and she was sure Brady did, too, that the hose part was unscrewed. The fumes were bad enough from where she stood. She had no idea how he could lean over it like that.

"And just what were you planning to do with this?"

"I wasn't planning anything. I told you it's not mine."

"Mmhmm." Sheriff Brady made a show of looking around the dark alley. "Then whose is it?"

Summer kept her mouth shut. She didn't know if she could trust the sheriff. He'd been huddled in the corner with Drew, Jennifer, and Mario at the dance.

Then she remembered seeing them chatting with Mrs. Beesley at one point, too. Maybe the sheriff already knew exactly who and what this was about.

———

Summer nearly pushed back against Sheriff Brady's hand as he led her through the station, back toward the same interrogation room she'd been in before. But this time she didn't like the feeling she got in the pit of her stomach. The place was much creepier at night, with the shadows making their way inside. Though, she didn't think that was what had her so wound up.

This time, even though she wasn't cuffed, she might as well have been. Summer had the sneaking suspicion she wasn't getting out of here this time.

"Sit tight. I'll be back to get your statement." He moved toward the door, then stopped. "If I were you, I'd really consider my options right now. This is your last chance to come clean...about everything."

He didn't say what everything was, but they both knew. Being caught behind a business with a gas can looked bad. Being caught behind a business that the owner publicly refused to sell to you, a week after being accused of a murder, looked guilty.

Summer wasn't sure how long he left her sitting there. All she knew was, when the doorknob turned, she was happy to see him.

Only, it wasn't him.

"This is rather disappointing," Mrs. Beesley said. She was still in her dress from the Fall Ball, though her heels had been switched out for some flats.

"Mrs. Beesley, I didn't do anything. I swear it."

"This is an awful lot of coincidences racking up, and not in your favor." Mrs. Beesley closed the door behind her and stepped closer. "Was my job offer not good enough?"

Summer opened her mouth, then shut it. She glanced sideways at the long mirror, then back at Mrs. Beesley. "I promise you. It's not what it looks like." Then the woman's words played in her mind again. "And you're right? It doesn't make any sense, does it? You offer me a job and *then* I decide to burn your place down?"

Poor Mrs. Beesley gasped and stepped back at the true gravity of the situation. Of what she nearly lost tonight.

"I promise you, it wasn't me."

"Then who was it?"

"I don't know," Summer lied. This time she didn't dare look at the two-way mirror. "I couldn't tell who it was. Only that they seemed to be up to no good. I went back there to get a better look and that's when the sheriff showed up."

There was a loud knock on the door that startled Mrs. Beesley. "For your sake, I hope that's the truth."

Sheriff Brady came into the room as Mrs. Beesley was leaving. "I've got the paperwork in my office for you to sign."

Mrs. Beesley paused, then set her shoulders. "That will not be necessary."

"Gertie, I don't think you-"

"That...will not be necessary," she repeated, and was gone.

Sheriff Brady turned on her, a dark glare in his eyes. "You seem to be the luckiest little criminal in the world, Miss Snow."

"Or innocent."

"Mm, well, guess we'll find out, won't we? I've got my guys on the scene now. Tell me, is there any reason your fingerprints might show up on that gas can?"

"Nope."

There was a commotion down the hallway and both of them recognized Carl's voice at the same time. "See," Sheriff Brady said, "lucky."

If you consider a murder charge and now possibly an arson charge to be lucky, then yes. Summer had the good sense to only say that one in her head.

"Ronnie," Carl said in his loud, booming voice as he barreled up the hallway.

"Carl, you know better than..."

"Sorry. Sheriff Brady," Carl corrected, giving the title the gravity afforded the president. "I've come to take Miss Snow home."

"And why would I allow that? These are serious charges."

"That Gertie just said she wasn't pressing..." Carl stared the sheriff down, though Brady was at least a head taller.

"For now. I'll talk some sense into her."

"Until then." Carl put out his hand for Summer to take. "She'll be under my care."

Sheriff Brady barked a laugh. "She was under your care when this happened!"

"That was my fault," came another loud, familiar voice. This one filled Summer with two warring emotions.

Evan's face appeared over Carl's shoulder and he smiled brightly at her.

Relief coursed through her veins, followed quickly by anger. "You're supposed to be watching my aunt!"

Another laugh from Sheriff Brady. "Yeah, there seems to be a lot of that going around."

"She's with my sister...spilling all your trade secrets to Daisy, I'm afraid. You're gonna have some competition in the Crazy Christmas Hair contest."

Summer didn't have the heart to tell him that all she wanted right now was to get on a plane and get as far away from here as possible.

"Brady," Carl said with a nod before grabbing Summer's arm and pulling her out of the station.

"So, what did you learn?" Evan asked when they were in Carl's car.

"That you don't follow directions and you're a tattle-tale."

Carl laughed. "Not really tattling when I could see you driving off in a bright yellow bug plain as day."

Evan gave her a look one might get from a righteous sibling in the backseat.

"Still, you left Aunt Clara alone. There's too much going on in this town. She needs protection."

"You try telling her that, then." Carl looked at her through the rearview. "She demanded I take her to her car, but she couldn't find her spare key. We'll worry about that tomorrow. What about you, kid? You alright?"

Summer hesitated before answering. It was the first time tonight she had a chance to actually take stock. "I don't think Mario's the killer. Or Frank."

"Well, good to know you're alright, then." Carl winked at her through the mirror.

"Have there been other suspicious fires in town?"

Evan started to say something, then looked up at Carl. After a nod passed between them, Evan answered. "A couple."

Summer leaned back in her seat and took a deep breath. "Well, if Marsha Peterson found out...maybe threatened to tattle-tale. That sure sounds like a motive for murder."

Evan grinned, then nodded. "Yeah, but for who?"

"Who had the most to gain? Jennifer or Drew? Or both?"

19

S ummer stood atop the steps to her aunt's RV, bracing herself for whatever was about to happen. Aunt Clara had an adventurous streak, but this probably pushed even her wild nature a bit too far. She had rehearsed a bit in the car, preparing for whichever version of her aunt was waiting.

When she opened the door, what she saw was nowhere close to what she'd imagined.

Most of Aunt Clara's belongings had been destroyed during the break-in. So what was left didn't take up much room. After redecorating, Aunt Clara had said that at least now it would be easier to pack up when it was time to hit the road.

Which was exactly what she was doing. Aunt Clara shoved her knick-knacks in a box, not stopping to wrap them or even place them gently.

Summer was about to ask what was going on when she saw the look on Aunt Clara's face. Then she saw the gun.

Jennifer was sitting on the small couch, pointing a sleek black gun at Aunt Clara. "Faster!"

Her demand made Aunt Clara speed up, and it made Barney start barking and growling from the back room.

Summer felt a movement behind her and realized Carl and Evan were about to shove their way in. She slammed the door and locked it.

Evan and Carl began pounding on it immediately.

Jennifer pointed the gun at her and waved it at Aunt Clara. "Help her."

Summer moved slowly and began pulling dishes out of the cabinets. She wasn't sure exactly what you had to do to get an RV road-ready. She just hoped there was something heavy she could get her hands on.

When the pounding on the door stopped, Summer knew they'd be back. She also knew that if she didn't do something soon, all of them would be in danger.

Jennifer's trigger finger looked awful twitchy.

———

"This was the dumbest thing you could have done," Summer said. Which struck her as funny because saying that was the dumbest thing she could have done. But now that it was out, she rolled with it.

She closed the cabinet. There was nothing throwable in there, anyway.

"You were getting away with it. Sheriff Brady suspected us! And now with the fire..."

Jennifer's gun followed Summer as she moved to another cabinet. She caught sight of Evan and Carl out the window. They waved frantically for her to let them in, but she kept going.

"The fire is why I'm here," Jennifer finally said. "I knew you wouldn't talk, not right away. And I knew that bumbling idiot wouldn't figure it out on his own. But it was only a matter of time. So I figured I needed some insurance."

The gun turned to Aunt Clara.

"Tell me!" Summer said, a little too loud. But it worked. The gun turned back to her. Along with the barrel of the gun came a familiar sound. The clank of Jennifer's many bracelets. It triggered a memory, and Summer slowly pulled her phone out of her pocket. "How could you do it? Your own mother?"

"You think I'm stupid enough to just let you record my confession?" Jennifer motioned with the gun for Summer to take her hand out of her pocket.

"I'm not recording anything." Summer unlocked her phone and swiped through her pictures. "Yep, just as I thought."

"What?"

Summer turned her phone around for Jennifer to see, then zoomed in on the picture. "I took this the night of the contest. Something about it always stuck with me, and now..." Summer tapped the screen. "You see that? Behind Aunt Clara? That's a hand reaching for the hair dryer."

"So," Jennifer shrugged.

"So, I think Sheriff Brady might be very interested in finding out just who belongs to that hand. You know, the one with all the bracelets?"

Jennifer switched the gun to her other hand and placed the guilty one behind her back. "Circumstantial."

"Maybe. Or...the smoking gun."

"Delete it!"

"Leave."

Jennifer couldn't make up her mind who to point the gun at now. It kept swaying back and forth, and she began muttering under her breath. "Couldn't leave well enough alone...Just one more deal. That's all I asked for. Just one more..."

"She didn't want to sell the park?" Summer asked, gently. She needed to lower the tension in the room.

"An apartment complex would have been perfect for this spot. I could have bought her out. She'd already messed up my last two deals. Getting soft in her old age."

Aunt Clara laughed. "Your mother was at least ten years younger than me and I still have a lot of troublemaking time left."

Without warning, Aunt Clara leapt for the gun.

There was a click and Summer froze, worried about what she might see or feel. But when nothing happened, she moved on Jennifer. Summer and Aunt Clara tackled her, wrestling on the couch until the gun went flying and Jennifer stopped struggling.

When they finally got her subdued, the door swung open with a loud crash.

"Dang it!" Aunt Clara yelled. "I just fixed that thing!"

"Technically," Carl said, "I did."

Summer got off Jennifer and leaned over to whisper, "You and Harding are going away for a long time."

Jennifer laughed. "Harding? Please. He's too dumb to pull this off. He was just getting in the way. And if this salon deal didn't go through, he was next on my list."

"Good to know," said a deep voice from behind Summer as Sheriff Brady darkened the doorway.

20

Three Days Later

Aunt Clara put Barney on the couch, a little too close to the box of knick-knacks. "You be a good boy and watch those while I secure the cabinets."

Barney sniffed the box, decided there was nothing interesting in it, and hopped down.

"You sure you don't want to come with me?" Aunt Clara asked, tying the cabinet handles together.

"So that's how you do it..."

"Don't avoid the question."

Summer took a deep breath. This had been the elephant in the room since the arson attempt. Now that Summer had no reason to stay, she had nowhere to go. It would have been easy to just tag along with Aunt Clara, but that didn't feel like her path.

"Pretty sure three's a crowd," Summer said, teasing.

"Carl has his own camper, thank you very much." Still, the dark red of Aunt Clara's cheeks made Summer smile.

"I'm sure Mom will be happy to let me crash in my old room for a bit. I think it's a gym now, but from what Dad says, it's more like a ghost town."

The only place she knew for sure that she wouldn't be—besides here—was back home. Not that Atlanta had felt much like home for a while.

Aunt Clara, likely reading the look on Summer's face, said, "They'll catch him."

Summer hadn't told her aunt...or anyone...just how much trouble she'd gotten herself into with Mr. DeVilla, but she couldn't stop the headlines from getting more and more ominous with each passing week. The longer DeVilla was on the run, the longer Summer was, too.

Too bad she had no idea where that would be.

There was a knock on the door, though neither of them were in a hurry to answer. Too many surprises had been at that door lately.

Barney, though, had no such reservations. He excitedly barked and scratched at the newly remounted door.

"It's Sheriff Brady," said the now too familiar voice.

Still neither of them moved.

"It's good news!" He sounded a little peeved, but also a little amused.

Summer opened the door and let Barney sniff at the sheriff's shoes a bit before scooping him up. "Come on, you can help me pack."

"What can we do for you, sheriff?" Aunt Clara asked, gesturing him in.

"I wanted to come by and give you an official 'all clear,' seeing as how you're about to hit the road."

"Thank you. We appreciate it, don't we, Summer?"

"Mmhmm," Summer said. She busied herself with folding shirts and shoving them into her suitcase. Somehow, they didn't seem to fit as well as they had on her trip into town. She leaned over and scratched Barney behind the ear. "Seems I'm gonna need you to sit on this thing for it to close." She patted his round belly and gave him a kiss.

"I'd like to thank you as well." Sheriff Brady came closer. "Not sure we would have gotten to the bottom of this one so quickly if it weren't for your help."

Again, Summer only answered with a noise.

"And I want to apologize."

At that, Summer looked up. "For?"

"I can't say I was too hasty, not with the circumstances. You have to understand what it looked like from my point of view. The murder with your blow dryer...then you standing right beside a gas can in an alley..."

"Apology accepted?" Summer said slowly.

"The apology is for the damage it might have caused to your reputation. I know you were in talks to buy the salon."

"I wouldn't say 'talks,' considering Harding wouldn't give me the time of day. And I don't think being cleared of attempted arson is enough of a resumé booster to get me my job offer back. Especially when that arson was *at* the place I was applying."

Summer folded her last shirt and dropped it in her suitcase.

"Well, maybe let's not be too hasty about that. Gertie's a reasonable woman and..."

Summer and Aunt Clara both made a noise that time.

"She's reasonable and...according to my sources...more eager to be out of that place than she might let on."

"Really?"

Sheriff Brady shrugged. "OK, maybe 'eager' isn't the right word either. But I think I can talk to her and at least get your job offer back on the table. It's the least I could do."

"I don't know," Summer said, though she was already daydreaming about long days at the salon, followed by a coffee float and... She swallowed and cleared her mind of what she'd been thinking. She couldn't let some guy she just met cloud her judgment.

"She'll stay!" Aunt Clara held out a hand toward Summer. Dangling from her fingers were the keys to the punch buggy.

Suddenly, Summer felt like she'd just been set up...again.

"Take 'em. I won't be needing it. Carl's car has heated seats. Way more practical for a ski trip, don't you think?"

Summer didn't reach for the keys, so Aunt Clara dropped them into her hand.

"Aunt Clara, I can't..."

"Nonsense. I told you before you even got here that you'd love this town. And I just know this town will love you back."

Summer tried to ignore the wink, but its hint was not lost on her. She shook her head. The last thing she needed right now was to complicate her life with...whatever that wink implied.

Aunt Clara picked up Barney and gave him a big squeeze. "You want to stay here, don't you?" Barney yapped and licked her nose. "See! It's settled."

Summer looked back at Sheriff Brady and her aunt. "I guess it's settled."

————

"Great, hope you enjoy your stay," the chipper woman behind the counter said as she handed Summer the key to her new room.

"Thanks," Summer said, taking the key and the mountain of brochures that promised The Manor House Inn was centrally located to all the best tourist traps.

The thought reminded her of Alex, who ran the cute sock store not too far from the Inn...true to the brochures' word. *'I'm craving chocolate waffles'* she texted Alex.

'I thought you'd never ask!'

'Same time?'

Alex replied with a thumbs up emoji and Summer dropped her phone into her pocket. She was looking forward to making a new friend, though she wasn't looking forward to her next meeting.

She had gotten a call from Mrs. Beesley earlier that morning, just as she was seeing Aunt Clara and Carl off. It seemed Sheriff Brady had been true to his word, and now she was about to find out how good—or bad—that conversation went.

The salon was dark when she arrived. And empty. The same strange feeling she had that night behind the alley crept up her back. What was she getting herself into?

"Mrs. Beesley?" Summer asked, quietly. There were boxes stacked along the wall and the shelves were bare. This was not a good sign.

Mrs. Beesley came out of the back room, holding a broom and dust pan. Her face was flushed and there were smudges all over her dress, but her beehive still stood tall. The sight of it eased Summer's nerves. Things couldn't be that bad if Mrs. Beesley had time to perfectly coif her hair.

"Ms. Snow," Mrs. Beesley said. "Thank you for meeting me on such short notice."

"Of course. Though...I'm not sure..." Summer looked around the near empty room.

"Yes, that." Mrs. Beesley set the dust pan on the nearest counter. "It seems I may have been a bit too hasty."

Summer raised an eyebrow.

"Now, I can't say for certain I *knew* you were innocent...of the attempted fire. The murder? I had a bad feeling about Harding all along."

Summer didn't bother correcting her, to say that it was Jennifer who killed her own mother over money. Or that Harding would have been next on her list. It was all still so fresh. And word would get out soon enough, anyway.

From what Sheriff Brady had said, Jennifer had confessed to everything. Not that she had much choice, considering the near full confession she had already given in the RV. Between that and the incriminating picture of her gaudy bracelets taking the blow dryer, the case would be pretty cut and dry. Soon the headlines would be everywhere.

"But you didn't want to take any chances," Summer offered.

"No. I did not. Regardless of who wanted to burn this place down...it worked. I couldn't have my employees or clients in here if—when they decided to strike again. So I closed up shop." Mrs. Beesley looked utterly dejected. Summer realized just how much she must love this place and why Drew and Jennifer had been driven to resort to such drastic measures to get rid of her.

"And now?" Summer asked, gently.

Mrs. Beesley stomped her foot. "Now I don't think I want to give that scoundrel the satisfaction."

Summer's heart began to soar. Maybe staying here was actually going to work out. It was such a lovely little town, one she could see herself putting down roots.

And somewhere like this was the last place DeVilla and his goons would think to look for her. She knew she couldn't outrun them forever. She only needed a little more time to get the proof she needed. As much as she had hated running around town and chasing clues to clear her aunt's name, it was a skill she knew would come in handy soon.

She smiled at Mrs. Beesley. "I think that's wonderful. I can tell you love it here."

"Yes, I do. And...I know this might not be what you hoped for. But I'm not ready to let this place go just yet. I built this salon from the ground up. It's my baby, now that my kids are grown and out of the house. I don't know what I would do with myself every day if I didn't come here."

Summer's heart faltered. She'd had it all wrong. Mrs. Beesley called her here to officially rescind the job offer. She was right back where she started. "I understand. I'm sure I can find..."

"I hope you'll at least give me six months."

"Excuse me?"

"I was thinking about your vision for the place. The flowers everywhere, lights up on the walls..." Mrs. Beesley pointed to the far corner where Summer had once imagined a large light feature. "I think it's just what this place needs."

"I...don't understand..."

"How about we make a deal? You come work for me, and we fix this place up together. Then, in six...seven months or so...I sell it to you."

"Really? Oh, Mrs. Beesley, that sounds amazing! I would love to! You won't be sorry!"

"I better not be."

Summer wanted to run to Mrs. Beesley and hug her, but the older woman was clearly not the sort. Instead, she reached for the broom.

"No, no." Mrs. Beesley pulled it away. "It's the weekend. Go...do weekend things. We have three weeks before our grand re-opening. Plenty of time to get your hands dirty."

Again Summer wanted to hug her. "Thank you. I do have a few loose ends to tie up."

"Yes, so I've heard." From the expression on Mrs. Beesley's face, Summer could only imagine what she'd heard. News traveled fast in a town like this, especially when her own aunt took it upon herself to spread that news.

21

Evan's shop was full of customers, though most of them seemed to be huddled at the counter. When Summer got close enough to see what all the excitement was about, she smiled.

Somehow, Evan and his niece, Daisy, had fashioned a tiny apron around Barney's ever-growing middle. Now, her cute little puppy was even more adorable, with his long, floppy ears hanging over a little name tag.

"Summer!" Evan clapped his hands and came running. "Our new mascot is quite the sensation!"

She did her best to ignore the warm glow that spread through her chest at his use of the word, 'our.'

"That's got to be the cutest thing I've ever seen. I need to take a picture!"

"Daisy's already taken a thousand. I'm surprised my phone hasn't self-destructed."

Summer waved at the little girl who was snapping several more as Barney swiped at the tiny paper hat she'd just put on him. "I thought they were supposed to leave yesterday."

Evan grinned. "Rosie couldn't tear her away. Something about refusing to leave her new best friend." He nodded toward Barney. "They're gonna stay a couple more days until her puppy fever wears off."

"That's great. I'm sure you're happy."

"Yep! And...what about you? Did you take the offer?"

Summer rolled her eyes and shook her head. "There really are no secrets in this town, are there?"

Evan shrugged. "Apparently, more than we realized. But not this one." He looked at her, waiting.

A huge smile spread across Summer's face. "Yes. I took the offer."

"I'm so glad. I couldn't bear to lose...Barney...so soon after meeting him."

Summer's cheeks burned. "Funny, he was just telling me the same thing. I'm glad you two found each other."

"Me too!" Evan suddenly looked away, then at the ground. "And I guess you'll be happy to stay...and see the case through to the end." He added that last part in a rush as if he'd only just thought of it.

"Honestly, if I never hear one word about the case ever again, it'll be too soon."

"Yes, I suppose you've had your fill of excitement."

"You have no idea!" It was Summer's turn to look at the floor. The last thing she wanted was for Evan to find out exactly how much excitement she'd had in her life lately.

Nobody could ever find out.

She took a deep breath and dug into her pocket. "You know what I am looking forward to?"

"What?"

Summer pulled out the coupon book. "Painting this town red!"

Evan's face lit up, then he looked from her to the coupon book, then back.

"Yes, with you, silly!"

The End

Afterword

Thank you for reading Hair Today, Dead Tomorrow. I really hope you enjoyed reading it as much as I had writing it!

If you have a minute, please consider leaving a review on Amazon, GoodReads and/or Bookbub.

Many thanks in advance for your support!

A Short Cut to Murder

About A Short Cut to Murder

In Spring Harbor, not all cuts are cosmetic.

In the picturesque town of Spring Harbor, where the scent of blooming flowers mingles with salty ocean air, hairstylist Summer Snow knows that beneath the surface of this idyllic community lies a tangle of secrets.

When a seemingly random stranger meets a tragic end in what authorities quickly label a mere "car accident," Summer's intuition—sharper than her best pair of scissors—senses a darker truth.

A cryptic text message from one of her regular clients days before the fatal incident becomes the elusive thread that Summer believes could unravel the mystery. With the town buzzing with whispers of tragic misfortune, she dives into a covert investigation, snipping through lies and weaving her way through a labyrinth of deceit.

As Summer navigates the twists and turns of this perilous pursuit, she must tread carefully. Will her determination

About A Short Cut to Murder

reveal a hidden killer lurking amidst the town's shadows, or will her relentless quest for justice make her the next victim?

A Short Cut to Murder
Sneak Peek

S ummer's fingers shivered as she begged the water in the wash station to warm up. Why anyone would want to get their haircut right before Christmas was beyond her, especially in this weather. But the salon was full, and the phone kept ringing. She guessed it was a good problem to have.

Tillie, the other stylist, twirled her dark curls in her finger, bouncing on one hip, as she spoke to a customer on the phone. Summer had been sure Tillie would have an issue with her coming in and changing everything...taking over like she owned the place already. But Tillie loved the ideas Summer had about the salon, so it made the transition easy.

Well, at least that part of it, anyway.

Mrs. Beesley came out of her office, scanning the room. Summer knew that look well. She was doing the math.

"Four full service cuts, two seniors, and a soft perm," Summer said, dipping her cold fingers in the finally hot water. She patted her customer, Marie, a beautiful woman with long, luxurious brown hair, to lean back.

"Plus two trims," called Tillie from the counter. She hung up the phone and jotted down the information on the new sign-in book.

Summer watched the sparkly pink pen glide across the page. It was the first of many upgrades she had made to the salon. Between that and the fresh paint—pale yellow with sea-foam green trim and rose vines between the work stations—the place looked like something out of a fantasy novel. Summer loved it, and from the uptick in bookings, so did customers.

Mrs. Beesley stepped farther into the room, but Summer put out her arm. "We have it under control. Don't worry."

Summer's phone buzzed in her pocket, rather loudly, and all eyes went to her. They had lockers in the back for personal items, but she rarely used hers. She couldn't bear the thought of leaving Barney with Alex for five to six hours at a time and not keep her phone on her. She wondered if this was what parents of actual human children felt like.

Mrs. Beesley came to the wash station, hands out. "Why don't I finish this for you while you get that?"

"It's fine," Summer lied. She was dying to answer it, but Mrs. Beesley was having trouble letting go of the day-to-day duties of the salon.

When the phone buzzed again, Summer knew she'd lost. Mrs. Beesley hip bumped her out of the way and started talking to the beautiful woman with the unbelievably long hair. "So, what are you in town for? The Light Festival?" As severe as Mrs. Beesley could be, with customers, she shined.

"No, but that sounds lovely." The woman's voice was husky, which didn't fit Summer's idea of her. From her tall, thin build and bright green eyes, Summer had pictured her with a perky tone.

Reluctantly, Summer pulled her phone out of her pocket and checked the texts, expecting the worst.

There were several alerts, but she went through the most important ones first.

'*Wish you were here!*' Aunt Clara sent a selfie with Carl in the background, trying to walk on skis.

'*Looks cold!*' Summer sent back with a selfie of her in front of the painted flowers.

Next was a cute picture of Barney with his left ear flipped back. The same one he always had trouble controlling.

'*Aww, I can't wait to get home*' she sent back to Alex.

Finally, there was a text from Vanessa. She saved it for last because Vanessa's texts were always hounding her to get back on social media, which she kept refusing to do. After that picture of Aunt Clara's hairdo went viral, people wanted more. Summer did not like the newfound popularity, not when she was supposed to be in hiding from her past.

'*This your guy?*' Vanessa's text asked, followed by a link to a news article. Summer opened it, expecting to see Evan's smiling face.

Instead, it was a full page feature on Drew Harding. His smug face stared back at the camera, arms folded like Superman, in front of a huge stage. Everything about it rubbed Summer the wrong way. Not only did he get in zero trouble over what happened with Marsha Peterson and the attempted fire at the salon, but now he was...guest speaker at a business expo in town.

Summer groaned and dropped her phone back in her pocket. "I'll take it from here," she said to Mrs. Beesley, just in time to sit the client up and wrap a towel around her hair.

"Everything alright with Barney?"

"Yes, he's fine." Summer resisted the urge to show her the cute picture. She was sure Mrs. Beesley had to be sick of constantly being forced to look at pictures of her puppy. "Actually," she said before thinking about it. "Did you know there's a business expo happening in town?"

"Yeah, starts tomorrow, I think. Everyone usually has a booth. I opted out this year, with everything going on." Mrs. Beesley wiped her hands on her apron and gestured toward the salon.

Yes, a lot had been going on these past couple of months. But things had to be calming down now. Nothing bad ever happened over Christmas.

———

"Right this way." Summer led the long-haired woman to her workstation in the far corner. She loved watching the season change through the window. Yeah, there were seasons in Atlanta, but not like this. Not the marked switch from fall to winter that she'd seen happen over the past few weeks here in Spring Harbor.

"That's so pretty," said the woman as she sat in the plush yellow chair Summer had convinced Mrs. Beesley to order.

"Right?" Summer replied, still looking out the window. But when she turned back to the customer, she saw the woman smiling at the circular backlit mirror in front of them. "They were not cheap, but I just had to have them," she added, thinking back to the long conversation she had with Mrs. Beesley about the purchase.

"Well worth it. You have an eye for design." The woman settled into the chair and immediately pulled her phone out of her pocket before Summer could wrap the cape around her. It was a signal Summer knew all too well. This would not be a chatty visit.

"Thank you! It's really starting to come together. So, what can I do for you? Trim? Bangs? I hear bangs are back in this season. All the winter hats. Need something to frame the face."

The woman unlocked her phone and held up a picture. "I want that."

Summer's mouth dropped open as she stared at the micro pixie cut. Her trance was finally cut short by a text pop up. She didn't mean to read it, but the weird phrase caught her eye.

'St. Patrick has left the cathedral' from Hank.

Summer looked away quickly, but something about the message stuck with her. First of all, it was Christmas, not St. Patrick's Day. And second, some guy named Hank didn't seem like the type who would be so invested in the holiday, or cathedrals. And third—the biggest and most glaring observation—that sure sounded like a coded message.

Visions of Secret Service men saying, "The Eagle has landed," into their radios flashed before Summer's eyes.

"Is there a problem?" The woman glanced at her phone and swiped the text away quickly. Her deep, husky voice that Summer had admired now sounded sinister.

Summer shook her head. She was being silly. Maybe she missed the excitement of the Peterson case and seeing Drew's picture had riled her up. "No, no problem. Sorry. Are you sure you want to go that short? All this beautiful hair...Oh! Are you doing Locks of Love?"

The woman—Summer found herself now trying to remember the name she'd seen on the sign-in sheet— thought for a moment before answering, "Yeah."

That did not instill confidence in Summer at all, but she went with it. "How long did it take to grow it out like this?" She finger-combed through the long locks, wishing she had the patience to do something like this with her own hair. "As soon as mine touches my shoulders, I'm looking for scissors."

"Couple years," the woman said, putting her phone back in her pocket. Clearly, there would be no further discussion.

Summer combed the woman's hair and sectioned it off with a scrunchie before holding up her scissors. "Last chance."

The woman flipped through a gossip magazine and gave Summer a thumbs up. All the while ignoring her phone buzzing away in her pocket.

Summer wondered if this was a messy breakup situation. She'd given many crying women a fresh new look while their boyfriends or husbands blew up their phones. Though none of those were in the dead of winter, and none intrigued her as much as this strange woman.

———

You can order your copy of **A Short Cut to Murder** at any good online retailer.

A SPRING HARBOR COZY MYSTERY **2**

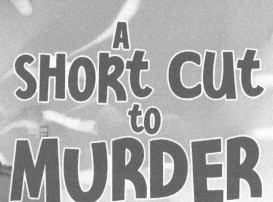

A SHORT CUT to MURDER

AMBER CREWES

Also By Amber Crewes

The Sandy Bay Cozy Mystery Series

The Spring Harbor Cozy Mystery Series

Newsletter Signup

Want **FREE** COPIES OF FUTURE **AMBER CREWES** BOOKS, FIRST NOTIFICATION OF NEW RELEASES, CONTESTS AND GIVEAWAYS?

GO TO THE LINK BELOW TO SIGN UP TO THE NEWSLETTER!

www.AmberCrewes.com/cozylist

9 798875 567131